EALRIS

D0321256

DEATHWATCH

SOMEONE IS WATCHING CAT McPHERSON.

Is it a young schizophrenic, a retired scientist, or Cat's ex-boyfriend? Or it could be someone else entirely. An obsession with insects seems to link them all. And Cat hates insects. She's easy prey, especially as she has given away so much about herself on an internet site which her parents have forbidden her to use. But does she even realize that she's being stalked? A talented athlete, Cat's too busy with the pressures of training and deciding whether she really wants to run for a living. The trouble is, soon she will have to run for her life…

A chilling and skilful psychological thriller, from the award-winning author of *Fleshmarket* and *The Highwayman's Footsteps*.

Books by the same author

Chicken Friend
Fleshmarket
The Highwayman's Footsteps
The Highwayman's Curse
Mondays Are Red
The Passionflower Massacre
Sleepwalking

Blame My Brain
Know Your Brain
The Leaving Home Survival Guide

DEATHWATCH

NICOLA MORGAN

EAST AYRSHIRE LIBRARIES	
451628	
Bertrams	25/03/2010
YA	£6.99

**WALKER
BOOKS**

This is a work of fiction. Names, characters, places and incidents
are either the product of the author's imagination or, if real, are used
fictitiously. All statements, activities, stunts, descriptions, information
and material of any other kind contained herein are included for
entertainment purposes only and should not be relied on for
accuracy or replicated as they may result in injury.

First published 2009 by Walker Books Ltd
87 Vauxhall Walk, London SE11 5HJ

2 4 6 8 10 9 7 5 3 1

Text © 2009 Nicola Morgan
Cover photograph © 2009 Brand X Pictures/Photolibrary Group

The right of Nicola Morgan to be identified as author of this work has
been asserted by her in accordance with the Copyright,
Designs and Patents Act 1988

This book has been typeset in Bembo, Justlefthand and Carnival

Printed and bound in Great Britain by Clays Ltd, St Ives plc

All rights reserved. No part of this book may be reproduced, transmitted
or stored in an information retrieval system in any form or by any means, graphic,
electronic or mechanical, including photocopying, taping and recording, without
prior written permission from the publisher.

British Library Cataloguing in Publication Data:
a catalogue record for this book is available from the British Library

ISBN 978-1-4063-1503-5

www.walker.co.uk

WITH SPECIAL THANKS ...

... to the wonderful Deathwatch Girls, my volunteer consultants from The Mary Erskine School in Edinburgh, who helped keep me on the right track with advice, opinions and enthusiasm from beginning to end. They were Astrid Batts, Gemma Bleakney, Jane Bryden, Caitlin Davidson, Emily Don, Mhairi Dunn, Rebecca Hughes, Ailsa Innes, Priya Khindria, Alison Lim, Abbie Logan, Kirsty Peters, Zoe Pritchard, Amrit Rattray and Bethan Riddell. Thanks and admiration also go to Diana Esland, the English teacher who gave up so much time and energy, and to Neil Dawson and the whole school for support in many ways. This was a really special project and it began not with me or any adults but with the girls' own enthusiasm when I first told them I was starting a book about a stalker.

Several members of the Patrick family, as well as Wilma Irvine and Sheila Fisken, helped with technical details of schizophrenia, swimming and athletics competitions, and how entomologists kill insects humanely. (No living creatures died or suffered because of the writing of this book.)

Oh, and to my niece, Lucy: next time you get a Madagascan hissing cockroach, warn your mother before you let it loose in the house...

CHAPTER 1
THE WATCHER
ONE MONTH AHEAD: OCTOBER

IN the hooded darkness, he watches from a high window. Staring into the night. October has begun and leaves twist and fall. Between the trees he has an almost perfect view of a nearby street, and one particular house, the one with the black door.

Sometimes he sees the people in it come and go. Then he knows when the house is empty. Or when only one person is in it.

It is someone he thinks about often now, perhaps too often for his own good.

He is reading his notes. Notes about many things. About everything in his head. Or almost everything. In a notebook with creamy, thick, unlined paper, which he has bought for exactly this purpose.

Some of the things he writes are painful to remember and hard to put into words. There is a wetness on his cheek. He brushes it away angrily and takes a deep breath, hardening his mouth and the muscles in his jaw. His eyes narrow.

He has almost reached the hardest part of his work. He feels in a hurry to move on but he must be patient. Precise by nature, he is military in his need for order, and things must be just right.

And now he has something else to consider, someone else. This has begun to intrude and to worry him. He wishes he did not need to think about it but he feels partly responsible. Guilty.

Trickles of rain run down the window. Stretching the stiff fingers of his left hand as if in pain, he touches the glass and traces the wriggling lines as they slither.

He stops watching and turns to something else. He needs a break from his note-making. There is something he had wanted to do earlier in the evening but he had made himself wait, tantalizing himself. Now he allows himself this small treat. He takes a pen with a good nib and begins to write slowly, on a small card, in well formed letters: Odonata Anisoptera *Libellula forensis.* And he blows the ink dry before placing it next to the insect sitting waiting in its plastic box: his new dragonfly.

He smiles. His insect collection has a new addition.

CHAPTER 2
INTRODUCING CAT McPHERSON
SEPTEMBER

ON the surface, life seems good for Cat McPherson. It is, you might say, perfectly imperfect – if it was perfect, people might be jealous of her. It has all the imperfections that keep her normal.

She is pretty, though she doesn't think so herself. She thinks her eyes are a murky grey, though someone more creative might call them steely dolphin blue; her nose, she thinks, is too long, though it isn't; she'd like her hair to be a paler blonde, even though many people pay good money for the colour that is naturally hers.

She's not annoyingly clever, though she can do well enough when she works. She isn't good at maths, but, let's face it, many people survive without being good at maths. She has all the normal worries, stresses, things to bug her, parents to say no to her more often than she'd like; but nothing she'd really need to wish away.

Personality-wise, she isn't perfect either. She's often

angry inside, or snappy or self-centred or wishes she was someone else or had different parents or more money or a whole new wardrobe. Or could eat chocolate without getting fat.

Pretty normal.

She has a younger brother — so, no, her life is *not* perfect. Perfect would be if he was older, and had fanciable friends who would fancy her. Instead of which, he's twelve years old, cocky and plays the saxophone, a lot, loudly, and irritatingly well.

Cat McPherson is known as a talented athlete. She's going to do it as a career. Everyone assumes. Her parents have nurtured this ambition. They are proud of their daughter's talent. What they don't realize is that the ambition is now more theirs than hers. Cat has had enough of the freezing early morning training sessions, weekends constrained by competitions or more training, loss of a social life, pulled muscles and feeling guilty about eating junk food. She is beginning to be irritated by being pushed and nagged or being told to read articles on sports psychology or books by Olympic heroes.

She's looking ahead — and whereas she used to imagine a life of medals and glory, now she sees regimes and injuries and not being allowed to eat rubbish if she wants. Winning is always important to Cat. It is part of her and gives her a buzz. But maybe that buzz is not enough.

She has not yet admitted this out loud. It is too new.

Well, she may have moaned vaguely about going to training on a rainy day or getting up in the dark for swimming, but her parents have not taken this as anything important. They have continued to push her, in a normal parenty way.

Besides, her grandfather was a brilliant athlete and all her life she has seen his trophies at her grandmother's house and been made to feel proud of him. He'd run in the Olympics, won a silver medal, and only injury had prevented him competing the next time and maybe winning gold. He died five days after she was born and his death was tangled in her birth. There's a photo of her tiny and screwed up in his arms, both of them in the same hospital, his eyes full of misty pain and pride and a huge smile on his face as though nothing would matter to him now that he had held her.

Cat's father is a GP and her mother a psychiatrist at the nearby psychiatric hospital. So they don't struggle for money, though at the end of each month they do wonder where it all went. They have avoided private school fees and they don't go skiing, but things still cost: the kids, two cars, meals out, an annual holiday, a large mortgage in one of Edinburgh's better districts, cosmopolitan Morningside.

It's an area where all sorts of people live side by side: writers and arty types, including some famous ones, alongside old ladies wielding walking sticks like weapons of mass obstruction as they battle their way into the charity shops; and frothy-haired judges, politicians, students, lecturers – all sorts.

It's a safe area.

You would think.

Cat lives in a tall, terraced, Victorian house. There are wooden floors, a Labrador, and a woman who comes to clean every week, wearing slippers and gliding around the house like polish, leaving behind her the scent of orange oil. The family eats together in the evening, though Cat's father is often not home in time: he comes back slightly tense and smelling of antiseptic.

Good, fresh food arrives on the table, usually cooked by her mother, who is not bad-looking, in a forty-five-year-old sort of way, and who will then spend the evening doing whatever women like her do.

Cat's bedroom in the loft conversion is decorated in two shades of purple and has an unused fireplace where Cat is allowed to put her collection of scented candles and incense burners. She has the usual technological gadgets, though not a television in her bedroom. And she's given up arguing about that one.

Her brother, though entirely capable of being intensely irritating, actually could be a whole lot worse. Besides, she is entirely capable of being pretty annoying in return. She practises hard.

All in all, even with the minor imperfections, you'd definitely say Cat was one of life's lucky ones. A winner.

Charmed, almost.

Safe.

Bad things happen to other people.

CHAPTER 3
FOOTSTEPS IN THE DARK

IN the darkening air of an early September evening, Cat McPherson breathed deeply. She shivered. Sweet tobacco smells floated from two smokers walking quickly home. A shout from her left made her turn – three winos fighting over a bottle of something. One saw her looking, and shouted abuse at her, before they all began laughing, or fighting: it was hard to tell.

Normal city life. Nothing new; nothing to fear.

She looked at her watch. Nine thirty. Late. Later than she should be. She often lost track of time when she was swimming, or she'd just do five more lengths, or ten, or whatever. Though it was sometimes an effort to get started, she had to admit that once she'd done a few lengths it became automatic, and even relaxing. And with a biathlon competition only three days away, she needed to do all she could.

Cat should have phoned home as soon as she left the

fitness centre. She knew that. Now she put her hand in her bag to find her phone. As she did so, it rang.

"Sorry, Dad!" Always better to get the sorries in first. "I was about to phone; I'll be home in five, ten at the most."

"I'll come and get you. Where are you?"

"No point. I'm on the main road already."

Actually, she wasn't. She was just about to walk along the edge of the park, but if she ran – which she planned to do – she could be home in five minutes. She didn't fancy waiting while he came. There was a cold breeze and her hair was damp. She zipped her tracksuit up to the neck.

Besides, if he came to get her he'd make such a big deal about how a) she knew she should have phoned for a lift and b) he'd had to make sure he hadn't had a drink in case she phoned.

"But I told you I wouldn't need a lift," she'd say.

"You can never be sure, Cat," her mother would say, taking his side, as usual. "It's always better to be safe."

But what could happen here? In the middle of Edinburgh, at nine thirty in the evening, with people near by? And streetlights.

She could outrun any attacker anyway, she reckoned. You didn't train every day, several hours at weekends, get selected for the Scottish Schools Athletics Association Under 16 team and win two medals at the last international competition, just to be outrun by some skinny creep who wanted your mobile phone. She could probably outrun most adults too, she thought. Adults were mostly unfit.

Her dad had been in the Territorial Army ages ago, before she was born; had been called up as a doctor in the first Gulf War and gone to Iraq: though he rarely talked about it and Cat found it hard to imagine him leaping off things on ropes or climbing over assault courses with branches sticking out of his helmet. If she was honest, she felt faintly ashamed that he'd been in the army, so she didn't think about it much. OK, so it wasn't the proper army, more a weekend activity for fitness and excitement, and none of them had really expected to fight in a war, he said, but still, it was army, and he was trained to kill. Not very nice. She was quite happy for him not to talk about it.

Anyway, if he'd ever been some macho tough guy, he certainly wasn't now. Her parents had both tried to go running with her one evening recently, after her mum had spent about half an hour deciding what to wear. Her dad had pulled a muscle on the corner of the main road and her mum, already out of breath, had said she'd go back with him. Yeah, right – as though he needed her help to go fifty metres. And Cat had carried on and returned an hour later to find them in the sitting room, most of the way through a bottle of red.

No, Cat McPherson wasn't afraid of being chased by anyone.

She checked that her bag was properly fastened, hoisted it onto her shoulders, and set off at an easy jog. She looked over her shoulder once – in the murky glow of the dim lights, two people were visible, one with a dog, the other a man walking quickly in the same direction as her.

Cat was not worried. Not then. Of course, she would keep her senses alert. That patch of trees would be a great place for someone to hide before jumping out on an unsuspecting walker. She narrowed her eyes, peering into the shadows. Her heart began to beat a little faster and she quickened her stride. There was a figure standing there. Just standing. He had a hood up but that didn't mean anything. Maybe he was waiting for someone and he was cold. She found that her hands were open at her sides, ready, waiting.

Cat could see the main road in the distance ahead of her, its lights and cars comforting. Not far away.

She focused on her pace. This was good, how she felt comfortable. In control.

That was when the lights went out. All the park lights. She could still see the lights of the cars in the distance but surrounding her was blackness. Unable to see the ground, she slowed to a walk.

Still, Cat was not really frightened. Annoyed, perhaps – another power cut. They'd had two or three during the hot summer. Some said it was the Council cutting the power off deliberately so that people would stop and think before using electricity.

She began to jog towards the lights of the cars ahead. She more or less knew where the path was anyway. Fear of tripping seemed less than the fear of ... well, whatever might be in the darkness. Fear of the dark was something normal, ancient, something you couldn't explain.

Footsteps behind her. Someone else trying to reach the road. Quite normal, quite easily explained. But she hurried, pushing herself beyond a steady stride, into something more pounding, her breathing faster, made faster by what was definitely now fear.

In the darkness, she couldn't run too quickly. She needed to see the ground.

She didn't look over her shoulder. One of the first rules of competitive running – don't look behind you – just *sense* your opponent.

Her phone rang. She couldn't answer it. It rang five times and stopped. She imagined her dad leaving a message, some instruction about where he'd meet her. He'd wonder why she didn't answer.

A noise behind her, sudden and strange, made her turn her head. A cyclist, the wavering light coming towards her fast. It swerved round her and sped on. Cyclists weren't allowed on this path, but people often disobeyed the sign – besides, in a power cut maybe normal rules didn't apply.

She could still hear the footsteps.

Her phone rang again. Logic took over: if someone wanted to attack her, they probably wouldn't do it while she was on the phone. And if they only wanted to steal her phone, they could have it. She stopped, pulled the bag off her shoulders, and fumbled desperately inside it. Grabbed the phone and pressed the button, peering into the darkness, eyes strained, every muscle alert. There was the figure coming towards her, with no more detail than a shadow. A bad runner, ungainly – but close to her now. She was ready to run again.

"Catriona, where are you?" Her dad's voice was sharp.

"I'm nearly at the road but…" She spoke loudly so that the other runner could hear.

"You said you were at the road! For God's sake, there's a power cut! And why are you out of breath?"

"Yes, I know there's a power cut! I'm in it!" The figure was close now. She still had no reason to believe he – she assumed it was a he – was actually following her or meant any harm, but the darkness was doing things to her mind. Her heart was racing and she *really* wanted to run. She had an idea. She whispered into the phone, "I have to go, Dad. I'll be home really soon." She pressed the button, ending the call, but shouted as though still speaking to him, "Yes! I can see your car!" Surely the man would not attack her if he thought her father's car was within sight? She began to run now, holding the phone as a torch.

The man was running too. She ran faster, faster and faster, her bag bouncing on her back, the phone light flashing to and fro as her arms pumped the air. The street was not far away, and she sped through the darkness, her muscles like springs, her fitness, speed and training the only things that would save her now. A horrible crawling sensation ran down her back, at the thought of him behind her.

Whoever he was, he didn't stand a chance, not against Cat's trained fitness. Soon she was at the main road, protected by the headlights and the people.

As she set off quickly towards home, heart still thumping and the cold air harsh in her throat, she looked round her, glancing behind, searching in all directions. But no one was following her. She stopped for a moment, staring at the few people walking along the pavements. A tall, thin woman, wearing a leather jacket, hurried towards a parked motorbike, climbed on it and sped round the corner with a practised roar. There was a young man, thickly coated, scruffy, a woollen hat pulled down over his straggly hair, his collar up, walking quickly away. Was it him? And even if it was, had he been following her?

No, silly idea, she thought. There's no way he was following me. It's just the darkness playing tricks. He would have had the same desire to get to the road as she'd had. Nothing to be suspicious about.

A cyclist, wearing a coat and hood but no helmet, came suddenly from behind the old police phone box a few metres ahead. He set off in the same direction as she was going, disappearing into the distance.

A few minutes later, Cat was in her small street. A loud motorbike went past the end of the street, briefly shattering the peace, but the noise quickly faded.

She turned her key in the lock. The familiar warmth and smells drew her in and she pulled the door shut behind her. A cyclist could be heard passing as she did so. A shiver ran down her neck before she closed the door firmly, and put from her mind all thoughts of her earlier fear.

Cat McPherson was safe.

CHAPTER 4
AN INSECT-LOVER

THE following day, an innocent September Wednesday. In the flickering unnatural twilight of the insect room of the National Museum of Scotland, a hand gently strokes the glass above the rows of beetles: *Coleoptera*. Beneath his fingers are legs, many legs. Thin, jointed, some of them long, some hunched as if ready to pounce.

Cerambycidae: long-horned beetles, with impossibly long antennae. Here, small and unobtrusive, is *Xestobium rufovillosum*: the deathwatch beetle. Some people say that it warns of approaching death. He hovers his hand above it, closes his eyes a little, tries to imagine. They are silly people who say this: it's a myth. The real reason for its name, he knows, is that this wood-boring beetle is often heard tapping in the floorboards and walls during the quietness around death, as people wait and watch in unusual silence.

Mind you, insects are clever enough: they *could* know

when death was approaching. He wonders what it would feel like to know.

As he moves to the next cabinet, there is a commotion. Through the door at the far end come some schoolkids with their teacher. Their silly, high-pitched voices grate, the girls squealing at an enormous model of a beetle. He clenches his teeth.

He must do what he has come to do. Replace the light bulbs in all cabinets where there is the sign: "Lighting failure reported by Visitor Services."

He doesn't need light. He's spent a lot of time here and could reel off the names easily. These are dragonflies, in serried ranks like army tanks or Chinese soldiers. Odonata Anisoptera.

Taking a special key from his toolbag, he opens the glass lid of the cabinet. He cannot stop a small smile, which seems to start from the pit of his stomach. It's a melting feeling, a softening as edges blur. When he has a cup of tea, he always holds the sugar-lump on the surface of the liquid and watches the tea rise into the sugar and dissolve it out of his fingers – this feeling is like that.

He needs to touch. And slowly, gently, hesitantly, he stretches his fingers towards his beautiful dragonflies.

He strokes them so softly that their dead gossamer wings barely shiver. With his eyes closed, he focuses all his senses into the surface of his fingers, feeling the invisible film of the insect fibres, his skin almost hearing rather than touching, the sensation as soft as breath.

Now he opens his eyes. It's a poor display, he often

thinks. Just the names, no information, and so much unsaid. So much more he knows. You can not tell from his brown coat, or from the fact that his task seems merely to be to change light bulbs, but he has been a professor of entomology – insects, to the rest of us. It has been his passion and life's work. He was once at the top of his profession, though not any longer.

"The most successful animals on earth" says a sign at the entrance to the room. And those kids, they know none of it. Do they know, for example, that dragonflies stalk their prey? Or that the male of the species is so well able to mimic the movements of its rival that its enemy doesn't even know it's being stalked?

He smiles. Such things make life rich and wonderful.

The kids are all assembled now and the teacher's strident voice breaks any chance he might have had to concentrate. He tries to shut out her words. And now the kids are coming nearer. They are so loud, so clumsy, so ignorant, so THERE. He glares in their direction, willing them to come nowhere near. Concentrating, needing to protect his insects now that their glass cover has been removed, he turns his body to shield them from prying eyes and fingers. Deftly he unscrews the faulty bulb and replaces it with one from his toolbag.

He is about to close the lid when, "Cool!" says a voice beside him. He jumps, his hand jerking away. A bitter juice of anger rises into his mouth. He snaps his head to the left and sees a boy standing there, sticky hair spiked, sweaty Biro-stained hands touching the cabinet edges.

"Be careful!" says the man.

But the boy has gone, laughing. "Chill, mister!"

The man takes several deep breaths. He closes the lid, carefully. He wants to apologize to the dragonflies, for disturbing their rest, but that would be foolish and so he does not. But he thinks it. He wishes everyone could appreciate them as he does. People should not be so ignorant of the astonishing cleverness of insects.

He goes to the next cabinet with a broken light. The kids are moving quickly from place to place, never focusing for long, interested only in how big, or how ugly, or how gruesome each insect is.

"They've got them bigger than that in London, Miss!"

"Look at its LEGS!"

"Oh wow, that one's EVIL!"

"Imagine finding that inside your shower!"

"I saw one like that in Thailand, Miss!"

And the squealing – God, the squealing! Won't they just shut up? He feels the rising of panic. His hands suddenly slip with sweat.

Two are looking at the cabinet next to him. He can smell them: washing powder and fried food. One hits the green button to turn the light on. Nothing happens, of course. Can't they read, the ignorant brats? The kid hits the button again. "It's not working, Miss!" And the kid hits it again.

He wants to tell the boy that hitting the button won't help, but the boy has run off to another display. The boy doesn't care what he looks at as long as he doesn't have to look at it for long. He has the attention span of a gnat.

But the other kid, a girl, is still standing there. He glimpses her and then forces his gaze to his insects, as he unlocks the cabinet lid. He repeats silently in his head, forcing his panic away with calming words, "Odonata Anisoptera. *Libellula forensis.* Odonata Epiophlebiidae."

Blonde hair, big hair, kind of swept back. Too much make-up. She is at least silent. She does not shriek and squeal like the others. He steals a glance again and that is when he sees it on her face.

Two things: hate and fear. She hates his insects. And she fears them.

He wants to tell her that she has nothing to fear, but he can't. He doesn't know how to talk to kids. Besides, nowadays, you talk to a kid and suddenly you're being accused of something horrible. And there's nothing horrible in his mind. Except a dislike of people. He likes insects more than people, much more. He understands and respects the creatures.

Ignoring the girl, he wipes his hands and gets on with replacing the bulb. And locks the lid again, wrapping his insects up. Protecting them, that's all he wants to do.

He concentrates on finishing his work, replacing all the light bulbs and removing the signs put there by Visitor Services. He has done a good job. He is not ashamed that this is his job, even though he has spent his life researching insects, has lectured in America and Australia in his time, has travelled the world with his work. But after his illness

– nervous exhaustion or breakdown it used to be called; stress they call it nowadays – he just didn't feel like going back to it, the lecturing, the constant demands to publish research. Then his wife died, and he'd opted out of life, and what a relief that was.

Now he spends his days quietly, caring for the collection, and other things in the museum, just to be there, just to breathe the air, with its faint and probably imaginary tang of formaldehyde. Occasionally he gives a talk to the nice ladies of the Women's Guild. Things like that. It's a soft and gentle life. And he likes it. Away from the pressure and expectation of success.

Back at the doorway, carrying his bag, he turns and looks at the kids. At such a distance he can watch them more easily. They flit from cabinet to cabinet, bashing green buttons. Silly kids. He doesn't want to be close to them. He hates children. Maybe that's a horrible thing to have in his mind. He finds them disgusting, primeval, uncivilized, ugly.

He has a moment of cruel pleasure as he recalls one of the traditional names for a dragonfly: the Devil's Darning-needle. So called because they are said to sew up the eyes and mouth of a misbehaving child. Some children could do with such a threat, he thinks.

Children frighten him because you can never be sure what they'll do. In a sudden flash of intuition, he thinks the girl must feel the same about the insects. His insects.

She shouldn't be frightened.

Not of insects. She should be frightened of other things maybe, but not insects.

She should be much more frightened of people than of insects.

The girl is still standing there. She begins to walk towards him. Or towards the door. Suddenly he recognizes her – he has seen her somewhere before. Does she live near him? Yes, he's seen her near by, definitely; maybe at a bus-stop or something. She is quite striking.

For a moment their eyes meet. Only for a moment, for they both look away. He is embarrassed, because he didn't mean to be looking at her and there was nothing bad in his mind, only recognition. She moves to the spider display – for there are spiders here, even though they are not insects – and he runs from the room, finding himself suddenly in a room with some pointless exhibition of data processing technology or something.

He will leave now, and go to his next task. Light bulbs in the bird room. Birds are boring, but they still need their light bulbs changed. Before he moves on, carrying his toolbag, he glances back.

She is standing there, her face screwed up in slight horror, as she looks at the bird-eating spider. Another girl joins her, with big eyes and thick, dark hair. The second girl speaks. "How does it eat the whole bird, do you think?"

He is out of sight now, but he hears his girl answer, "I don't think it eats it all in a oner."

And she is quite right, he thinks. Bit by bit the spider eats the bird. Bit by bit. It takes its time.

CHAPTER 5
MONDAY MORNING NEWS

CAT McPherson and her friends pushed their way through the mess of bodies towards the hall for assembly. Jostling and noise, the usual. Always louder on a Monday – so much more to say.

And today, today especially, there was plenty to say. News had spread of Cat's success on Friday. She'd won the under-16 age group at the regional biathlon competition. Biathlon was a tough discipline – swimming and running, using her body to its maximum – and not many people could do it, with its different demands on the muscles and body shape. She was still high on the feeling of winning, buzzing with it. It made the training worthwhile, made her think perhaps she *could* do this for the rest of her life. Though she'd probably feel differently next time she had to train in the rain instead of going shopping with her friends.

Anyway, as well as winning, she'd broken a club

record in the swimming, had personal bests in both swimming and running, and her face was in the papers today. Some of her friends' parents had seen it at breakfast. Several teachers had seen it too. The Deputy Head had already congratulated her. He had actually sounded quite sincere, and for one horrible moment she'd thought he was going to shake her hand. Mr Grime looked like some kind of leggy spider, with spindly legs that seemed too flimsy to support a body, tiny amounts of thin black hair, and an oddly protruding stomach.

One thing she didn't tell anybody. It wasn't that she deliberately didn't tell them. She had simply forgotten. It had happened just before the announcement of her victory, and the excitement of all that had put this incident from her mind. Well, it would, wouldn't it? After all, there must have been a few hundred people who watched her that day, so why would she remember particularly this one man?

But yes, she had noticed him. Not that she'd recognize him again – he'd had a hood up so she hadn't been able to see his face clearly or his hair. She had seen he was writing something in a notebook, standing apart from the other spectators. And she'd been sure he was watching her, maybe writing something about her. He'd been near the entrance when she'd come off the track. Her imagination had begun to take over: he could be a talent spotter for the national squad. She had felt a lurch of excitement. Even if she was not sure how much she wanted to be in the national squad, who would not want to be *asked*?

She'd seen him again afterwards. Talking on a mobile phone. And looking at her, she was sure. For a crazy moment, she imagined that he was phoning the Olympic selectors about her. Ever since she could remember, she'd had daydreams about competing in the Olympics and it didn't take long to conjure up that particular gold-medal-winning fantasy.

Or maybe the mobile conversation was to tell his wife he'd be late home for tea.

Anyway, then she'd got caught up in the congratulations and the excitement of winning. So she had forgotten about the man with the notebook. Completely forgotten about him.

Now they were all in the hall, finding positions on the floor, trampling over each other's feet. Bethan and Ailsa were on each side of her, Josh and Marcus messing around behind her, and others from her year all about. Bethan, loud-voiced, dramatic, dark-haired, was acting the part of her manager or agent. Priya and Alison and Amrit and the others all wanting to talk to her, be seen with her. The first and second years were looking at her. This was what fame would feel like.

Someone had brought the newspaper article and they were showing it round. Backchat, insults, laughter, messing about. She was fired up by excitement. There were few better feelings than winning.

There was a face she didn't want to see. Danny. She'd split with him during the summer and it still wasn't easy seeing him. He was looking at her now. If their eyes met, his always seemed to linger just a little long, seeming to say nothing at all, dead eyes, and yet the nothingness said everything. He was still angry, she knew. Or assumed. Well, she hadn't exactly treated him brilliantly, she knew that, but she hadn't fancied him any more, so it had seemed right to stop seeing him. And yes, she should have told him sooner, not let him find out from someone else. And she kind of regretted that, but what had happened had happened.

Mostly, they could go for days without bumping into each other. They were in different sets for most subjects. And he did all the sciences, whereas she only did one, because you couldn't avoid it totally. He was sciencey. It was one of the things they didn't have in common. There were a lot of things, actually. In fact, she'd started to go off him the first time she saw his collection. Insects. She shuddered.

Cat did not like insects or spiders. Well, why would you? What sort of a person kept dead insects in plastic boxes? And what sort of a girl would want to go out with a boy who did that?

Horrible brown things. Insects, not boys. With legs. More legs than a creature needed. And Danny kept them. He'd started collecting them when he was about ten, apparently, and those ones were a bit mouldy and their legs were somewhat curled up and not looking fully functional. They looked seriously dead. But others looked so well preserved they could have been alive. Those were the ones he'd bought. Bought!

What kind of a person BUYS insects?

You could laugh or you could shudder. Cat shuddered.

She'd pretended to be interested at first. After all, at that point she'd still fancied him. And she wasn't stupid – no way was she going to tell him she hated insects. She had a brother, and she knew very well what boys do when they know a girl hates insects.

Mind you, of course Danny had found out.

Anyway. Moving on. Life was too short to keep thinking about Danny. He'd get over it. He'd have to.

When her success was announced in assembly, there was a round of applause and cheers and whistles. Cat blushed, but enjoyed the attention.

Danny said nothing. But that was OK. There was no rule that everyone had to say well done. She hadn't noticed whether he'd joined in the clapping in assembly. Maybe he had; maybe he hadn't.

In pretty much every lesson, a teacher said something about it. It got to the stage when Cat wished they'd all stop. Friends could easily go off you for less than that.

When Maureen, the dinner lady, said, "Well done, hen! What a wee star!" Bethan and Ailsa groaned.

"Sorry," said Cat, as they took their trays to a table. "It's actually getting to me too."

"We're all just jealous really," said Bethan, with a grin. Bethan was not the jealous type. She had nothing to be jealous about anyway, not with those looks. Bethan oozed confidence, was never short of attention. She'd been Mary three times in primary school. That sort.

"Anyway, we're basking in your glory," added Ailsa. "Should we get your autograph now before you're too famous?"

"That's not going to happen," said Cat.

"How not? It could." Bethan nicked two chips off Ailsa's plate. "Though maybe not if you eat chips and slob around and get fat like the rest of us."

"Sometimes I'd rather do that."

"You saying we're fat?" demanded Ailsa, waving a chip in her face.

"You know I'm not! But it's starting to get to me. I don't think I can face a life obsessing about food and exercise."

"I thought you were really into it, the training and things."

"I don't know any more. I don't like the others at the club. There's, you know, bitchiness, and when I'm there on Saturdays I'm thinking about you all doing stuff without me. And when I'm swimming before school, you're all still in bed!"

"But you could be rich and famous," said Ailsa.

"And go to the Olympics. And we would know you! We'd have a famous friend!" Bethan added.

"But I might not. Most people don't get that far. Anything could happen." And as she said it she felt cold.

"Have a chip," said Ailsa. "With ketchup. It'll make you feel better."

Cat took one. The instant pleasure of a chip was too much to resist.

"Hey, I was going to be her manager!" said Bethan. "How can I manage a fat slob?"

They shared the rest of the chips. Afterwards, Cat was still no nearer knowing whether she'd rather eat chips or win races.

When school ended, they piled out of the gates, spilling into different directions, their uniforms marking them out as the same. Some at the bus stop going north, some at the other side of the road, going south.

Cat, Bethan and Ailsa joined Josh and Marcus as they climbed into the bus. Alison and Priya leapt on at the last minute with some others, and voices rose as they all talked about everything and nothing. Plans for homework, television, and as much time as possible spent on Phiz. Cat, of course, had an hour's training to do, but she didn't mention that – friends could easily get bored by things that didn't involve them. They couldn't really understand her dreams and fears. The twin dangers of obsession and failure.

She had noticed Danny as she left the school gates. He was on the other side of the road, watching her. He turned away and took out his phone and did something with it.

On the bus, she joined in the banter, putting any other thoughts aside. Losing friends would be worse than anything else.

Once off the bus, one by one the others disappeared into their own streets. Marcus was the last to turn into his road. They said goodbye and she walked on towards her own street. Her own front door.

Cat could see Polly on the sofa in the window. Cat smiled and mouthed "Bad dog!" through the window. Polly jumped down and was at the door as Cat turned the key in the lock.

"I'm back," she called, fending off the Labrador's wet nose.

Angus shouted through from the kitchen. "You got flowers! Someone loves you!" She went through to find him. Flowers? Who from? Angus, his dirty blond hair sticking up as if randomly but actually quite deliberately arranged, was making peanut butter sandwiches. She wrinkled her nose in disgust. He was cutting through a huge doorstep of bread with pale brown stuff oozing from the middle. He pointed over to the sink, where a small but expensive-looking bunch of flowers sat. She had no idea what sort they were, except that she did identify a couple of roses.

"Who're they from?" she asked, chucking a dog chew at Polly, who took it away to her bed.

"How do I know? There's a label. Mrs Morris brought them round when she saw me come home." Mrs Morris lived a couple of doors down and noticed everything. If she saw a delivery being made, she'd be darting out of her door, saying, "They're not in, you know." As if the delivery man couldn't work that out for himself.

Cat picked up the label that was attached to the

paper wrapping. "Congratulations," was printed on it. She turned it over. Nothing, apart from the address of a flower shop: Blooms.

Angus was looking over her shoulder. Breathing peanut butter over her. "So who is it?" He picked up the card, turned it over, his fingers grubby with everything he'd touched during the day.

"Piss off, Angus, you stink. I've no idea who they're from. Could be anyone." She was intrigued. Flowers were not normal.

She looked inside the flowers. There was no other card or message. Nothing except flowers. One of the roses was broken. Its neck was twisted.

First things first – she needed a snack before training. She knew perfectly well what she *should* eat, but she didn't. Life was way too short for slow-release, low-GI, low-fat, wholegrain, brown, cardboard food. She made a cheese spread sandwich, selected a seriously good chocolate biscuit. A cup of tea. Grapes. She put them all on a tray, ready to take to her room.

And now the flowers. She could take them with her upstairs.

She began to remove the wrapping. The scent was strong, amazingly so. She pressed her face into the petals.

It was Angus who made a noise first, a sort of small yelp of surprise as he pointed at her, at something on her shoulder, or her neck. He was grinning. Her scream came a split second later. She yelled, and flung the flowers away, screaming again. They flew in a high arc and landed, scattered, on the floor.

A huge spider fell from her shoulder to the floor by her feet and she sprang away, her heart thumping and her skin cringing. She had felt it tumble down her arm. Its legs were scrunched up beneath its bulbous body. It was dead. But Cat was not sure if it had been dead when it fell from the bouquet, or if the act of her brushing it away from her had killed it.

She screamed again, shudders tingling all along her spine, as though spiders were still scuttling over her skin. Her whole body felt cold, shaking, and she wanted to run from the room, even though the creature was obviously dead. Her face was screwed up as she kept brushing imaginary things from her.

Polly came running back into the kitchen. "Get the spider, Polly," said Angus. And Polly did. Labradors eat anything.

At that moment, their mother came home, saw the mess of flowers, and peanut butter sandwiches in the kitchen and took control.

"What lovely flowers!" she said, picking them up and gathering them expertly into an arrangement. "Who're they from?"

"She doesn't know," said Angus, who was grinning in disbelief at the amount of fuss one girl could make about a small dead thing. Cat was still standing far away from the flowers, pressed against the kitchen units, trying to recover some kind of dignity. It was, after all, only a dead spider.

Yes, a very large one – unusually large, one might say – but still only a dead spider. Harmless. Unless you were stupid enough to live in Australia, where such things were normal. Snakes, too. And leeches and giant wasps and other pointless things that would be better off extinct.

"Interesting. Have you got an admirer, Catty?"

"I've no idea!" she snapped. "Just make sure there are no more spiders in it!"

"Come again?"

Angus explained. "You see, Mum, there was a totally enormous man-eating spider that just leapt out and attacked her before she valiantly destroyed it with the force of her superhuman fear."

Her mother shook the flowers in exaggerated fashion. "Well, there's nothing there now. You're quite safe from dangerous creatures." She put them neatly in a vase and handed it to Cat.

Cat shook her head. "Just put them there; I'll take them in a minute."

"You want me to phone the shop and find out who sent them?" Cat nodded. Her mum picked up the phone and dialled the number on the card.

"Yes, hello. Can you help me? My daughter received some flowers this afternoon and there was no card saying who they were from… What about the name on the credit card … so you mean you have no record of the sender at all? … Well, can you remember if it was a man or a woman or how old or anything? … Well, could you ask her … yes, it's Diana McPherson." And she gave her phone number and hung up.

"Not much help there. The woman who took the order isn't in, and the flowers were paid for in cash. So no one knows. And they didn't sound at all interested. The man said he'd ask the woman who took the order but to be honest he didn't seem as though he was that bothered. I wouldn't hold your breath for them to phone me. I expect you'll find out, though – someone will ask if you received them. Meanwhile, they're lovely, aren't they? You should put them in your room."

Looking at them with crinkle-eyed suspicion, Cat took the flowers gingerly and put them on her tray. Up in her room, she cleared space for them on her dressing table. As she ate her snack, went quickly on Phiz and dragged on her clothes for circuit training, she looked at them every now and then, wondering who they could be from. The label had probably been accidentally dropped but she had some ideas who could have sent them: some likely, others less so. They could be from her club, or her trainer. Possibly. School even. Stranger things have happened.

Once she'd recovered from the shock, she didn't wonder for two seconds about the spider.

After all, it must have got there by mistake.

CHAPTER 6
THE FIRST DUEL

MAYBE Cat would get used to the mask, but at the moment she hated the warm black mesh round her face. It smelled of metal, and sweat from the padded cloth protecting her throat. She wished she could have her own fencing mask, rather than borrowing a school one, used over far too many years to protect far too many sweaty faces. She found herself breathing a little more shallowly than she should, her lips tightly closed.

Through it she could make out the other fencers, trussed up in the same stiff padded jackets, like the straitjackets she imagined her mum's patients wearing. Though her mum had often told her that none of her patients needed straitjackets. "Don't be a victim of stereotypes," she'd said. "I haven't seen a straitjacket used in years."

There was Ailsa, recognizable from the thick, dark brown hair hanging down her back. And Priya, model-tall and slim, complaining that the jacket made her look fat.

And there was Danny, just about to put his mask on. *Looking* at her. And then looking away.

She wished he hadn't decided to sign up for fencing. Surely he knew she had started too? Well, yes, and maybe that was why he'd joined. Or maybe it was a coincidence. After all, with a teacher like Mr Boyd, a lot of people were signing up. Mind you, that was mostly the girls. For obvious reasons: Mr Boyd was seriously good-looking. For a teacher.

As for the boys, some of them slagged him off behind his back – jealousy – but they still wanted to be in his class. Because Mr Boyd was a kind of sporting-hero type. Did extreme sports at weekends; had broken his nose playing rugby; had quadriceps that bulged like tree trunks; could climb up a rope with his arms alone. Had shown every new year group that particular trick.

Anyway, Cat had taken up fencing for a different reason. Her athletics coach had recommended it because it was part of the modern pentathlon – running, swimming, fencing, riding and shooting – and he said she should give it a go. Not many people could do pentathlon, he'd said, but *she* was special. And as soon as he'd mentioned it to her parents, she'd found herself persuaded to sign up for fencing. It was the word "special" that did it: their daughter, the star.

She wondered when riding and shooting would come into it. Absolutely no way! When she was younger she'd wanted to ride, but not now – too time-consuming.

Even more time away from her friends. As for shooting, well, it would be quite interesting. Different. But what sort of people would do it? Aggressive people. Weird types. She didn't think she liked the sound of modern pentathlon. Sounded like a load more training, as well.

She was going along with the fencing idea only because you had to take a Wednesday after-school activity and this term's options were fencing, cookery or drama. Cookery and drama didn't appeal. Cookery would be all health and hygiene, which she had enough of at home. She didn't like drama – that was Bethan's scene, ever the performer. Drama queen, in the best possible sense.

So she would do fencing, but forget pentathlon. They couldn't make her do it. It was her life, not theirs. She was the one who had to do the training.

Cat didn't like to think of their reaction if she confessed that she wasn't sure about a career as an athlete at all. Trouble is, she wasn't good at anything else. What else could she *be*? And if she threw away something that had been her dream ever since she remembered, what would be left? Who would she be if she wasn't "Cat, the athlete"?

And now Danny had started fencing too, three weeks in to term. She wondered what he was playing at. He wasn't your average sporty type.

Cat took the mask off for a moment and breathed deeply, though in the school gym the air wasn't exactly fresh. It was fetid, with feet and fustiness. Sweaty plastic mats. She retied her hair, tucking stray strands behind her ears. She pulled the huge suede glove onto her right hand and flexed her fingers stiffly inside it. Mr Boyd was handing out foils to a few pupils. "Here, Catriona, I'll put you against Danny. Go easy on him." He passed the foil into her gloved hand and she put the loop round her wrist.

Her heart sank, but there was no getting out of it. She had to pretend she didn't care.

"Salute each other, please. Remember?"

Masks under their arms, they did the ritual movement with the sword. Yes, well, it might be a sign of respect but it didn't change how she felt about him.

Now she placed the mask over her face, pressing the flexible back tightly onto her head. With her left hand she checked that it fitted properly, so that it could not fall off. All things she had been taught to do during the first two lessons. Not something you'd easily forget, not with a long metal sword – or "foil" – flashing in your direction. Even if it did have a hard plastic button on the end of it. She wondered if it ever happened that the button fell off.

She and Danny faced each other. This was Danny's second lesson and her third. His first actual fight. They nodded to each other as if in respect, as the rules stated they must.

At Mr Boyd's signal, Cat readied herself in the on-guard position, still feeling somewhat silly in the odd white breeches and long socks. But she soon forgot this as she concentrated on the details of the position: weight evenly on both feet, body upright, right foot pivoted round to face ahead, heels in line, left arm held at an angle behind her and wrist relaxed, whole body twisted sideways to present the narrowest possible target. And her sword-arm held softly bent in front, the foil steady, or as steady as she could make it. The tip pointing upwards, in line with her chest. Balance was everything.

She'd been practising this position in her bedroom, using a ruler as a foil, the mirror as a target. After the first lesson her thigh muscles had screamed for days. As Danny's probably were now. But now Cat's muscles, strong already, found the stance easy, natural. She smiled, hidden behind her mask.

Something rushed through her, unwanted, unexpected: the heady drug of competition. The need to win. She couldn't help it. It was deep within her. It was her.

"Best of three hits," called Mr Boyd and he gave them the signal to start.

She advanced, easily and fast. Danny moved forward too. Mr Boyd shouted something from the sidelines. Something to Danny, something about keeping his left arm up. Cat watched the point of Danny's foil, saw it wobbling. She smiled again. There was an advantage to these masks – no one could see what you were thinking.

She lunged. But Danny was too quick. He parried her foil and it did not make contact with his body. He lunged in return, only just missing her.

"Good riposte, Danny!" shouted Boyd, clapping.

She narrowed her eyes, aware of people watching; aware that many of them would know that this was Cat and Danny: Cat and Danny who until recently had been an item. Who had a history. Not that Boyd would know that, probably.

She was back on guard. And now Danny lunged. She hadn't expected it, not so fast. But she parried him, aggressively clanging his foil away. He lunged again, and the point of his foil touched her below the collarbone.

"Hit!" shouted Boyd. "Well done, Danny!" How could she have let that happen? Now she moved forward fast, two steps in quick succession. Danny stepped back, just quickly enough. Her arm was rock-steady; his was wavering. He was on the defensive. Her body fizzed, that drug rush again. Like anger and hunger rolled together.

But he had recovered, quickly steadying his feet, sending his body moving forward again. He lunged. She had to leap back and sideways and only at the last split second did she parry his blade. It brushed her arm, but hitting the arm did not count.

She had to win! Winning was what she did. And against Danny? All the more reason. With huge force, and fury, she lunged forward, under his foil, a dangerous move. He had not expected it, and shifted backwards, frantically stepping out of the way as her foil came towards his chest, towards his heart.

"Hit!" said Boyd.

She felt like shouting it herself as she sensed her blade

press hard into his chest. One all. Back to the on-guard position.

She lunged, quickly, without giving him the chance to think. She would not let this go.

He managed somehow to avoid her blade, but she pressed forward her advantage, lunging again, her face hot with rushing blood. Her foil just touched his chest. She'd won!

What happened next, she was not quite sure. Did he trip as the tip of her foil touched his body? Did the sole of his trainer catch on the floor? The next thing she knew was that Danny was flat on his back, looking like a stranded beetle, legs waving, his black mask still on his face.

And everyone was laughing.

Cat did not know why she did what she did next. It was a moment of madness, driven by the adrenalin that rushed round her body; the need to win; the pleasure of it. She stood over Danny and touched the point of her foil to his throat, looking down on him like some medieval knight with a victim at his mercy.

Mr Boyd came over. "Catriona, don't be silly."

Ashamed, she stood aside. Danny clambered to his feet. He was clutching his left hand. He must have fallen on it. Either that or he was pretending, as an excuse for having lost that bout.

"Remove your masks," ordered Mr Boyd. Her hair was stuck to her forehead. Danny's face was red, the cheeks moist with sweat. His eyes were furious.

"OK, we'll stop the bout there," said Mr Boyd.

What did he mean, stop the bout there? It was finished anyway. She'd won, hadn't she? She glared at him.

"That wasn't a valid hit, Catriona," he said, looking straight at her.

"It was! I felt it touch!"

"You know the rules – the foil has to bend. And it didn't."

"It did so! Come on, Sir!"

"No, Catriona. I'm the referee. And I didn't see it. And you know what they say about the ref's decision."

"But…"

"No buts. Where's your sense of sportsmanship?"

"Sportswomanship," called someone.

"Of course. Sportswomanship," Mr Boyd said, no expression on his face. "Or maybe even sportspersonship. Whatever you call it, Catriona, you of all people should know about it. Fencing is a sport, not a war. Catriona?"

"Yes, Sir."

"I'll fight on, Sir. I'm fine," Danny mumbled.

"No, you're not. You've hurt your hand. Let me look at that."

Catriona could see that Danny's fingers would not straighten properly. Mr Boyd called for someone to get an icepack from the first aid room and made Danny sit down on a bench at the side while the others set to work practising moves.

She went over to him. Without looking directly at his face, she managed to speak. "Sorry about that. Are you OK?"

"Sorry about what?"

"I don't know … for making you fall over."

"You didn't make me fall over. I am quite capable of falling over all by myself without any help from you." She said nothing. He continued. "You're not that great, you know. I scored the first hit, after all. You think you're so great at anything you do. Well, get used to it – you didn't win just now."

That stung. It bit in the guts, set her stomach clenching. She tightened her jaw.

"Danny, we went out for a while. Big mistake, hey? Get over it!" And she turned and began to walk away.

"Over it? How up yourself can anyone be? I am so over you, you wouldn't believe it."

The rest of the lesson went badly. She lost two bouts. OK, they were with pupils who had done fencing last year, but still. Losing does things to you. It can make you angry. Sometimes that's good in competition, but sometimes it's not. Winning depends on dealing with losing.

She won some bouts too. And Boyd gave her praise, but it felt hollow. She tried not to look at Danny again. Someone came with an icepack and Cat was aware of the fussing round him. She looked over once. He was watching her.

Why had she ever gone out with him? Because his

smile, when he used it, was gorgeous, in an unusual, crooked sort of way. And because he had been nice to her, flattered her. And they'd had a good laugh together. Yes, well…

But then, of course, there'd been the time he'd stood her up. Some family thing that got in the way. And he'd said a couple of things about her being posh. So she'd been embarrassed to ask him round to her house but he'd pestered and then he'd come and all he could do was look at things like the blatantly expensive kitchen and the books everywhere, and the cleaning woman had been there, and she'd wished she hadn't let him come.

Then there were the insects. Actually, the insects had come first. It was after she'd looked so obviously turned off by his insect collection that things had started to go sour. The visit to her house had been later. He'd told her that her bedroom looked like a palace.

"Shame you're no princess!" he'd joked. What did he mean?

Anyway, she'd responded quickly, "At least I don't get off on dead flies."

And it had been pretty much downhill from then on.

Why did life have to be complicated?

But he would get over it. He'd have to. If she just ignored him, just pretended nothing was wrong, he'd soon get bored.

CHAPTER 7
BAD FEELINGS

CAT'S dad looked hunch-browed and dark-eyed, giving her a row just because she hadn't taken her mugs down from her bedroom. She *never* took her mugs down from her bedroom without being told at least five times, so what was the difference now?

Her mother was no better. Tight-lipped and silent in the kitchen as she chopped vegetables aggressively. Scowling when Cat came down with six mugs in varying stages of congealment hanging from fingers and thumbs.

"Just put them there. I'll do them. They'll need to soak before going in the dish-washer."

"Dad said I was to do them." Cat clanked them down a little too hard on the granite work surface, before starting to run the tap.

"Just leave them, Catriona! And why can't you bring them down as soon as you've used them? Why do you have to wait to get a row?"

Cat was silent. Obviously they were in a bad mood. Did she care why? Parents *were* ratty sometimes. It would be something that would blow over soon. Might make for an uncomfortable meal with both her parents black-faced and tense for the start of a weekend. But hey...

Though probably not a good time to say that she wanted to cut down her training at least for a while. She'd rehearsed it in her head, but she hadn't found the moment.

Cat didn't give much thought to why they were in a bad mood but it wasn't long before she found out anyway. Later that evening she was coming downstairs to get some milk when she overheard their voices in the sitting room.

First, her dad's voice, "I wish to goodness you'd listened to me and not written the damned thing."

Her mum's voice came back, bitter-brittle, "As I said at the time, I couldn't afford not to. Professionally. Leave it, Bill – it's not something we're ever going to agree on, is it?"

"But I've seen the patients. The symptoms are there – and they're not all psychiatric."

"Oh, please – let's not go over all that again! Can't we just agree to disagree?"

"Not if you're going to keep raking it up by writing journal articles that could get noticed by the newspapers. And then by some pressure group."

Cat paused outside the door. Her mother's voice came now.

"But I've seen the research, hundreds of thousands of words of it. It's clear that Gulf War syndrome has a psychiatric basis. Post-traumatic stress, shellshock, whatever we call it: you know the arguments."

"Yes, but you're only reading the psych research. And I was there myself. I saw…"

"Yes, Bill, I *know* you were there. I *know* what you saw. I've been married to you for sixteen years, remember. I've heard your stories and they're horrible, of course, but—"

"God, Diana, you sit there in your ivory tower and you haven't a bloody clue! I have three Gulf veterans in my own practice with symptoms that are not psychiatric. I see rashes and joint pains and—"

"Bill, please. Let's not do this again. I wrote the article, as suggested by the department, because it's what I believe and because if I hadn't I'd have had to explain why. And do you think I should have said, 'Because my husband says I mustn't'?"

Silence. Then the clink of bottle on glass.

Her dad's voice. "What if a newspaper picks it up? What if one of my patients notices it? My professional connection with the barracks is important to me. Life's too short to fight other people's battles for them. It's not as though this is your big crusade – why can't you stick to schizophrenia?"

"Come on, we've talked about this before; we're always saying I should diversify. You know how I feel sometimes, seeing the same type of patients every day, knowing that in too many cases I can't help them. Well, this was a chance."

"Fancy being a GP?" asked her dad. "Snotty-faced kids and fat people? Diarrhoea, eczema and piles?"

"Not particularly!" There was a slight laugh in her mum's voice, though it was strained, as if she'd been close to tears.

Cat went towards the kitchen now, her thoughts mixed, glad they weren't arguing any more. But her mum had sounded low. Adults didn't seem to have that much control over their lives and dreams either.

Cat didn't know exactly what Gulf War syndrome was, though she'd obviously heard of it – the last time her mum and dad had argued about it. Some kind of illness or disability that a load of soldiers got and people argued about what it was and whose fault it was. It seemed very irrelevant to her. OK, so her dad had been in Iraq during that war, but even that was history. Before she was born. There'd been another Gulf War since then, but wasn't that supposed to be over? She didn't really know, only that both her parents agreed that this one had been wrong. But how did you have a *right* war? Weren't wars just one of the ways people messed up the world?

Time to stop thinking about it. Her parents were not getting divorced or suffering from a terminal illness, and there wasn't anything else to worry about.

Back upstairs, Cat switched off her parents and logged on to Phiz. She knew she should have been getting ready for bed, but she was never sleepy until much later at night.

Anyway, everyone else would be on Phiz, and she might miss something. And that guy might come back tonight and put himself on her PhizPlace. For her to choose.

Would she take the risk? Would she say yes or no? Hot or Not?

One of the best things about Phiz was the risk factor. All the other sites were so up themselves, full of rules to avoid perverts listening in, all rules set up by paranoid adults. They should realize that most people her age were perfectly capable of staying safe online. Only idiots would get into any kind of danger.

Parents seriously didn't approve of Phiz, which was another point in its favour. Newspapers were always going on about it. Her dad had read something out about it from the *Guardian* and asked if Cat used it. She said she didn't. He believed her... And the police had recently made some statement warning parents about it. All of which added to the attraction.

So Phiz was adult-free, unlike the other networking sites, where you'd suddenly find that a teacher had joined.

Her parents didn't know she used Phiz, obviously. It was a simple matter of one click to hide the page if they came into her room and she'd always have an innocent page open behind it that she could switch over to. Homework or something.

Back to the cool guy.

Phiz was about watching people. That was where the newspapers got the idea of stalking, but it wasn't stalking. After all, you *allowed* yourself to be watched – it was all with consent. And watching and being watched was the whole point. You went on the site and browsed for people you liked the look of – from their hobbies or messages or tastes or whatever on the public pages. When you found someone, you would sign in as a watcher and hang around before making contact. You played games with people when you were a watcher. You kept them guessing. At each visit you had to drop a new hint about yourself, and after a few hints the person being watched had to decide whether to say Hot or Not. Of course, the watcher could have lied. But it wasn't really dangerous; you wouldn't actually meet them. You wouldn't be so stupid.

And you could have lied about yourself too. You had an online identity, which could be anything you wanted. A perfect version of yourself, maybe. You without the spots, big nose, thin hair, whatever you didn't like about yourself. Touched up photos, if you wanted: there was a touch-up facility on Phiz. DIY plastic surgery. It was called Celeb Me. Cat had made her nose smaller. Smoothed away her arm muscles to make herself look a bit thinner. Made her hair a bit blonder.

So this guy had been watching her. Which gave her a shiver of excitement. She'd no idea what he looked like, of course: *he* was watching her, not the other way round. He would be able to see her pictures on the public part of her page.

Incidentally, she was assuming he was a guy. She'd said in her profile that she was straight, so she guessed he would be too. Otherwise what would be the point?

She was interested in him – the clues he'd put about himself were definitely right. He'd put a picture of running shoes first of all, which got her interest going. Then swimming goggles. Which got her interest going again. Now, earlier this evening, he'd put something new up.

A fencing mask.

That thrill had rushed through her. In her imagination, he must be sporty, fit, otherwise why the sporty clues? She'd no idea where he lived but that didn't matter because she wasn't going to meet him. She'd no idea what he looked like either but she could dream.

Now, after three clues, she should decide whether to let him into the secret parts of her page and put him on her PhizPlace. That was a commitment. Like going out with someone, except less time-consuming. Phiz relationships didn't interfere with training.

And you'd never have to admire his insect collection.

First, though, she'd ask her friends. She clicked on their symbols. But only Bethan was there. The chocolate bar was her symbol. Cat went into the personal message section and wrote: *"hey!! hes intrested! 3rd clue a fencing mask!! well?????"*

The chocolate bar started melting: Bethan was replying. In a couple of seconds, the reply came: *"hey u could play it cool for a bit u dont no much about him yet"*

"whats to be sure about??? i can just zap him if it doesnt work"

"how about u ask more?? theres nothing to lose"

Cat felt a twist of irritation. Wasn't Bethan on her side? OK, so Bethan didn't have a Phiz relationship going just at the moment but friends were friends, no matter what. And Bethan wasn't the jealous type. She was probably just being cautious. Cat would probably have said the same. But she didn't want caution.

She typed: *"it'll be fun!"*

"go for it then but b careful. keep me posted. gtg – homework calls groan xoxoxox"

Hesitating just a little, Cat clicked the button that said Hot. She had a brief horrible moment when she wished she had waited longer, wished she'd listened to Bethan's caution, but now her page fizzed into life: stars and fireworks everywhere. Her heart was racing as the guy's Phiz symbol came twisting onto her page. Along the top, as always, were the symbols of her other friends who had full access. But the person you had in your PhizPlace would always have pride of place – top right-hand corner – and whatever you were doing on your computer, his symbol would always be there. Watching her.

In a moment he would appear there, and she waited to see what he would have chosen as his symbol.

It was taking ages for his information to load.

Nearly finished.

She peered at the screen. It seemed to be going grey. Dissolving almost. Flickering. The mouse was frozen too. All the pictures along the top were fuzzy at the edges.

Was this normal?

CHAPTER 8
PHIZ

A sound behind Cat made her jump. Someone was coming. She spun round, twisting the laptop away so that her mum or dad wouldn't see it.

"Angus! DON'T come in without knocking! Creep. Piss off!"

"You're on Phiz, aren't you?"

"So? You do it too. Now just get lost, will you?"

"Can I borrow your KJ Martin CD?"

"No."

"Please."

"Don't get anything disgusting on it or you'll have to buy me a new one."

"Where is it?"

"For God's sake – here. Now, seriously, piss off!"

She threw the CD case at him and he caught it easily.

"Thanks. And, hey, sis, take a chill pill, why don't you?"

When she glared at him, he retreated, shutting the door.

She turned back to the laptop. Looked at the screen.

And gasped, her skin going cold as the blood rushed to her heart. The whole screen was taken up with one picture. An enormous spider, its legs almost furry, its eyes still and staring.

Watching her.

Cat shook the mouse and the spider shrank into the corner, occupying the PhizPlace icon. Her screen now looked normal. But her heart was still racing. All her concentration was focused on the screen. Something horrible was happening and she had no idea what it was.

She clicked on the symbol and quickly started typing into the message space.

"hi nice to meet you but i hate spiders. can u change your symbol? PLEASE!!!!"

Silence.

She typed again. *"look sorry but i really really hate spiders!"*

Nothing.

She felt cold. A chill crawled down her neck. What had she done? Who had she let into her computer?

But she knew who it was. It had to be – Danny! Danny knew she hated spiders and insects. Danny obviously knew she had started fencing. And Danny was angry with her. Danny would do something like this.

"danny?"

Silence.

"I know its u. Why are u so pathetic?"

"I'm not Danny."

"who then?"

Silence.

Of course it was Danny.

"who are you?"

Silence.

And now, cold inside, Cat realized something: she actually hoped it was Danny. Because if it wasn't, who was it?

"Cat? Are you in bed? Computer off? Light off in ten minutes." Her dad's voice.

"OK."

A few moments later, there was a knock on the door. Her mum and dad. Cat minimized the window, instantly replacing it with her homework – though she couldn't help noticing the spider still watching from the corner. She made a huge effort to turn towards the door with a blank and easy face. As though nothing was wrong. Inside, her thoughts were a storm of confusion. Every sensation was concentrated in her head, until it pounded.

"OK for the morning?" her mum asked. There was a sort of extra brightness in her voice, fake. But Cat just wanted rid of them.

Meanwhile, her heart sank. The morning was Saturday biathlon training. Including a friendly competition between the club members and a few invited from other clubs.

She'd almost forgotten. On purpose. It would be cold and her friends would be doing something without her.

But now was *definitely* not the time to have the conversation...

"Yes, fine." As quickly as she could, Cat got rid of her parents, managing to say good night in such a way that they would not notice anything wrong. Her dad lingered briefly, as if wanting to say something, but Cat glared at him. *"What*, Dad? I'm busy."

"No need to be rude," he said, his voice even, before saying good night and leaving.

"Computer off *now*," repeated her mum as they disappeared downstairs. "I'll come and check in ten minutes."

"OK!" Cat knew her mother wouldn't come and check. Mild fake threats were standard parent strategy.

Her breath released slowly in the emptiness. Back to the screen. She clicked on the symbol.

The spider filled the screen again. It was grotesque. She felt her face screwing up. But she needed to know.

She clicked on the message bit and typed, her fingers tripping over each other: *"so who are you? and sorry but if you dont get rid of that spider then your dumped."*

"That's not very nice. I heard you were properly brought up."

"Your not very nice."

"You don't know that."

"OK, you are dumped. sorry but i made a mistake. you messed me around lets call it quits."

"Quits? I don't think so!"

She wasn't having any more of this. Whoever he was – and she still suspected Danny – he was horrible and she didn't want to waste her time. She began to zap him, dragging the spider symbol towards the Phiz Dump Bin. As she pulled him towards the bin, relief swept through her. There was nothing to fear from Phiz. Getting rid of unwanted attention was this easy.

Win some, lose some. Never mind. More fish etc.

But as she reached the Dump Bin and let go, the spider span back up into the corner, where it sat, watching again. It seemed to breathe, pulsing slightly, as though it could spring at any moment. Frowning, she tried again. Maybe she'd just let go too soon. But once again, the spider refused to be dumped. Now it appeared across the whole screen again, huge, monstrous, before shrinking to its watching position in the corner.

Cat's heart began to race again. Her armpits were damp.

"Come on, come on," she muttered, as she dragged it one more time to the Dump Bin.

This time the spider slid into the bin and did not crawl back out. Cat waited for a few seconds to be sure.

No problem. She had no idea why it had been so difficult. She'd never deleted anyone before and maybe this was a feature of Phiz. Maybe you *had* to try three times, so that you didn't accidentally delete someone. Or she just hadn't dragged it properly.

Whatever, he was gone now. If it was Danny, she'd

find out sooner or later. It must be him. Who else would be so creepy?

Well, a creep, of course. And there were more creeps in the world than Danny. Maybe one of them had found her. Maybe that's what adults were so paranoid about. Well, they were wrong: she'd got rid of him.

When she began to close down the computer, an error message came up – "The programme is not responding" – and then came code numbers. She tried again. Nothing happened. The screen was frozen. Only one solution: crash the system. She kept her finger pressed on the power button. It seemed to take a very long time to switch off, but eventually, of course, it did.

Blackness. Silence. She breathed deeply.

Cat put the laptop away and got ready for bed. With the light off, and her alarm set for the morning, she lay trying to sleep. She could not get the picture of that huge spider out of her mind. Even with her eyes closed, it was still there. Watching her.

Eventually, sleep came. But at some point during the early hours, the spider entered her dreams. She woke, wet with sweat, her heart racing.

As she reached for a glass of water, Cat McPherson told herself not to be so stupid.

Just a creep and a picture of a spider. Nothing that could possibly affect her if she didn't let it.

But, in the dark, alone, it's not that easy. She pulled the duvet over her head. No good. Its voiceless rustling was worse than silence. She plugged her iPod into her ears and listened to anything: she didn't care what. As the rhythms drummed into her head, she let herself be taken away by the music, holding onto the notes.

She forced the spider guy from her mind.

And, much later, fell asleep.

CHAPTER 9
THE CANAL

CAT and Angus were walking along the canal with Polly. A thin low sun scattered through the trees that Saturday afternoon and Polly was annoyingly interested in the smells along the waterside.

"Hurry up! Stupid dog!" shouted Cat. She wanted to get back home. Too many things to do. She and Angus were supposed to walk Polly once a week, though they usually managed to get out of it. No getting out of it today, though, not with parents still in crabby mood – her mum had been phoned first thing in the morning by some journalist wanting a comment on her article and her dad was giving her the "I-told-you-so" treatment. And Cat and Angus had been subjected to the "parents-being-reasonable-and-seeming-to-tell-their-kids-everything" chat at breakfast, during which Cat had had to pretend she hadn't overheard their conversation about it already.

It had turned into a full-blown debate, with Angus siding with their mum because she'd stood up for her beliefs and Cat feeling the need to side with her dad who was saying how terrible it was that soldiers risked their lives for their country and then found that their injuries, whether mental or not, were dismissed. And it's really not what you need at breakfast when you're about to go to athletics and run in some boring so-called "friendly" competition. And what competition was ever friendly? Then her mum had made her wash up, which Cat suspected was some kind of petty revenge for having sided with her dad. And to cap it all her dad had said he couldn't take Cat to athletics as he had golf and she had to get the bus because her mum was taking Angus to buy new saxophone reeds because he had *suddenly* realized he had no spares.

The day had continued as lousily as it had started. She'd run badly in the unfriendly competition and had had to deal with sarky remarks from her trainer. So what with parents and trainer, plus Phiz lingering at the back of her mind, not to mention the fact that Angus kept playing air sax as though he thought he was a famous player – something to do with a concert coming up, which no one was allowed to forget – Cat was in no mood for Polly sniffing everything instead of walking properly.

A scruffy barge or houseboat or whatever they were called was moored on the near bank. The sun was behind it, blinding Cat as they approached. She didn't know if she'd seen it before. She'd never looked that closely at the boats that came and went, and sometimes stayed, along the canal.

Cat wondered what it would be like to live on a houseboat like that. *Did* you live on them? She didn't know. Maybe you just had them as places to get away from your family. Or maybe you went on trips or holidays. Where did the canal go? Glasgow? She didn't really know that either.

The vessel didn't look particularly well cared for, its green paint peeling and a rusty chain hanging from the small deck. The long, low cabin formed most of the length of the boat, a pot of fresh flowers sitting at one end, and a metal ladder up to the roof. Also on top of the cabin, dominating it, was a motorbike, partly covered by a tarpaulin. That was what made Cat notice the barge in the first place – you didn't expect to see motorbikes on boats.

The tiny deck at the front was filled by a woman sitting on a chair, watching them as they approached. She had a notebook on her lap, a mug of something on the deck beside her, and a bag of crisps in her hand. A pack of cigarettes and a lighter lay beside the coffee mug.

Cat felt observed by her. The woman really was staring. Hadn't she ever seen anyone walking a dog before?

Then the woman raised her hand, as if waving. It seemed as though she might be about to speak to them.

Cat wanted to pass her as quickly as possible. She wasn't in the mood to make pointless conversation with some stranger. Unfortunately, Polly had other ideas. The bag of crisps was to blame. Polly identified the crunchy sound and the crackling of the packet. She went and stood near the edge of the bank, wagging her tail wildly. Any moment now and saliva would be hanging from her mouth.

"Polly! Come here!"

Polly stood where she was, wagging her tail even more vigorously, suffering a sudden attack of selective deafness.

"Polly!" shouted Cat again, embarrassed.

Then the woman threw a crisp, which Polly caught. *Great*, thought Cat. *Now we'll never get away.*

"How old is she?" asked the woman.

"Six," said Angus.

"Labrador?"

"Yes."

"Lovely dog. I was thinking about getting a dog. For company. Would you recommend a Labrador? Maybe a bit big on a houseboat?"

She seemed to want to talk. It must be lonely living on a boat. She looked about fifty, though it was hard to tell because she was scruffy, her straggling hair the colour of metal streaked with rust.

The woman looked … what? Fragile, Cat thought. And sad, sort of. Her long body was folded into the chair like a crumpled fan. She was thin, in body and face, her cheekbones sharp. There was a small mark on her face, the thin white line of a scar on her cheek. Maybe she had been attractive when she was younger, but it didn't look as though she cared about that now. It must have been months since she'd seen the inside of a hair salon. And fashion was clearly not her concern.

But it was her eyes that were striking. They gleamed from a dry-skinned face. They seemed to hold the light. It was hard not to look at them, but Cat felt uncomfortable. Pierced by them.

"We should get back," Cat said to Angus. "Come on, Polly, time to go. Nice meeting you," she said to the woman, with a polite smile.

"Indeed," said the woman, staring at her as though she knew how keen Cat was to get away. "Nice meeting you too. Goodbye, Polly. Maybe see you again, eh?" And she waved.

"Weirdo," muttered Angus to Cat as they turned away.

And they carried on along the towpath.

Cat found herself thinking about the woman, wondering about different people's lives, how they turn out. When the woman had been fourteen, as Cat was now, did she imagine that in thirty or however many years' time she'd be living on a cramped, grotty boat with peeling paint and the silty stale smell of canal? Maybe she never wanted to settle down with a normal job, promotion, money, family. But what if she'd had other dreams?

Maybe the woman *was* a weirdo. Or maybe she was just sad.

Cat had a gut-wrench of fear. About her own future. She'd always been told that if she tried hard she'd be successful, have a good life. But now she wasn't so sure. Maybe it wasn't that easy. And besides, here she was contemplating giving up the thing she'd dreamed of.

Everyone talked about career choices. But how much choice would she really have? How much control?

She hurried along the canal after Angus and Polly, and tried to put the woman out of her mind.

CHAPTER 10
AN INSECT MAN VISITS

BIOLOGY. Not Cat's favourite subject. And today's lesson looked like being worse than normal. Every now and then the school got a random expert in to talk about something from the real world. This time it was an entomologist. Someone who studied insects. A weirdo, in other words.

Cat was feeling lousy that day anyway. Not the best weekend. After the Phiz incident, she'd slept badly, woken tired and gritty-eyed, which explained why she'd run badly on Saturday. Then they'd gone to see her grandparents in Fife for the night, come back on Sunday afternoon to pouring rain and so much homework to do that she'd had no time to go on Phiz. Actually, she'd tried to, late at night on Sunday, but her laptop was playing up, going slow, had to be rebooted twice before it would work properly, and then her mum had insisted on turning the wireless router off downstairs because it was bedtime.

So the weekend had been the pits from beginning to end. Monday morning had a lot to recover from. And it had been really hard to get up to go to her early morning swimming, with the house dark and damp. When her swimming coach had come to the house to collect her as usual, she'd kept him waiting for five minutes and he'd not been best pleased.

Miss Bleakney had apparently told them about this insect talk after the lesson the previous Friday, but Cat hadn't been there because she'd had to show some new parents round. So it had come as a surprise when she'd arrived at biology on Monday morning to find this odd, nervous-looking man, with his very thin hair carefully draped over his shiny head, standing beside Miss Bleakney and taking small plastic boxes out of a crate. She was helping him, holding them up every now and then and exclaiming.

"Ooh, a dragonfly! Isn't it stunning!"

"Yes, indeed, indeed. Odonata Anisoptera *Libellula forensis*, of course," said the man, taking it from her and placing it softly on the bench.

"Of course," agreed Miss Bleakney. As if she knew.

Some of the boys and a couple of girls were crowding round, jostling. One tried to touch one of the boxes but the little man became instantly agitated. "No, please, please, no! Don't touch!"

"But they're dead, aren't they?" said Marcus.

"Oh, quite dead! Naturally, they're quite dead. But fragile, very fragile."

"Sit down, please, class! Rebecca, Jonathon, Neil, you too! Priya! Amrit! Amrit, for goodness' sake!" snapped Miss Bleakney.

They obeyed, though noisily. Cat, Bethan, Emily and some others sat at the furthest possible table, their faces slightly screwed up, a little tensely, wondering what on earth was the point of this.

Ailsa came and sat at Cat's table, squeezing in beside her. "This makes a change," she said. "Better than Bleakney."

"You think?" said Cat. "He looks creepy."

"Now, class." Miss Bleakney was clapping her hands, her long straight hair tied back severely, her white coat clean and starched, her trendy, rectangular glasses halfway down her perfect nose. "Settle down. I would like to introduce you to our special guest, Professor Bryden.

"Professor Bryden works in the National Museum of Scotland, where we visited recently. He is an expert on insects. A very distinguished entomologist. He used to go on terribly exciting expeditions to exotic places around the world, collecting insects." It was hard to imagine this balding, shiny man in any exotic place, but there you go. Professor Bryden blinked rapidly from behind his glasses like a gecko.

"Professor Bryden is now retired from his academic career, but he works part-time at the museum." Miss Bleakney beamed excitedly. "And now he has brought some of his insects to show you. I am sure we are going to find it fascinating and, who knows, perhaps there's a budding entomologist among you! Please put your hands together and show your appreciation in the usual way."

And everyone clapped loudly. Some even cheered, which flustered poor Professor Bryden. His tongue flickered in and out a few times before he started speaking.

Cat concentrated on not looking at the insects. She listened to what he had to say – after all, there'd probably be a test or an irrelevant task for homework – but she tried not to look at the creatures as Professor Bryden picked up each box and described the contents. She was glad she was sitting near the back.

The funny little man was actually not a bad speaker. He started off nervously, making what he probably thought was a joke to get them relaxed, but he hadn't learned that his sense of humour was ancient.

Anyway, very soon, Cat sensed the class become still, listening carefully to his words. Though it pained her to admit it, he had some quite interesting things to say about insects.

Termites, for example. Those towers they built – they weren't designed for living in, and they weren't accidental either – they were air-conditioning systems to bring cool air down into the hot African earth. And bees – bees were amazing. Apparently, bees could count the number of wing beats their friends made and they'd know where to go to get the nectar. Bees danced for a reason. Dragonflies were interesting too – they actually stalked their rivals, he said.

Trouble was, then things changed. Professor Bryden asked if they'd like to hold an insect. A live insect. A cockroach. A Madagascan hissing cockroach. Dictyoptera Blaberidae *Gromphadorhina portentosa*, as he announced.

A murmur went through the room. Dizziness swam through Cat's head. She breathed deeply, glancing at the door out of the corner of her eye. She, Emily and Bethan looked at each other, their faces screwed up. Ailsa was looking scarily keen. But then, she *was* sciencey.

Professor Bryden took a large plastic box out of the crate. It was about thirty centimetres long, about the same tall and a bit less wide, with condensation on the sides. Inside was a rotten log. At first, she could see no insects, until something moved, something brown, which she hoped was a piece of bark but rather obviously wasn't. It was also unpleasantly large. Still, as long as it stayed a long way from her, impersonating bark, this was absolutely fine.

She was aware that more than one creature was in the box.

"Cool!" said someone.

Professor Bryden smiled at these eager faces, relaxed now that he could see their interest. He continued, "So who wishes to hold one?"

CHAPTER 11
THE MADAGASCAN HISSING COCKROACH

A load of hands shot up. Not Cat's. Nor Emily's. Nor Bethan's. The boys who hadn't put their hands up straight away soon did. With the girls, it depended. It was a personality thing. Cat would normally want to join in with whatever was going on, but since she had zero desire to hold a cockroach, whether hissing or not, she stuck with the girls who stayed silent, their faces creased in distaste.

Danny's hand went up.

Ailsa muttered, "Not Danny. That would be cruelty to animals!"

Danny looked directly at Cat. Cat returned his gaze. "Your turn next?" His words were clearly a challenge. She could see it in his eyes.

She felt her heart racing. She had a horrible feeling that this lesson was going to turn out even worse than she'd feared. She still wasn't sure if it had been Danny on Phiz. But he knew her hatred of creepy-crawlies, and he would know very well that she didn't want to touch one.

Everyone had to wash their hands with some special substance, to protect the cockroach from germs. What? Weren't they the germiest creatures around? Professor Bryden was giving some explanation but Cat didn't listen. To say that she cared nothing about the immune system of a Madagascan hissing cockroach would be the understatement of the year.

Now several pupils held out their hands and amid exclamations and laughter they each held a vile brown creature. Alison, at their table, was obviously up for it, but Alison wasn't afraid of anything. Cat wished she wasn't sitting at her table, though at least she was at the far end of it. Cat, Bethan and some others stayed quiet and waited for it all to be over.

Cat concentrated on breathing, slow and deep.

Why would anyone want to do this? The horrible thing sat there, antennae waving, crouched on tiny legs. When Professor Bryden touched the shiny brown back, a sizzling noise came like cold water poured on a hot roasting tray and everyone shrieked.

Miss Bleakney noticed Cat and her friends sitting silently. "Girls, none of you want a go? Any of you? You might regret it if you don't."

That seemed exceptionally unlikely.

"Yeah, come on!" said some of the boys.

"Go on! You're not *scared*, are you?" It was Danny.

And even if he didn't say so, she knew it was directed at her.

"No, Danny. But just because you can have a deep and meaningful relationship with beetles, doesn't mean we all have to," Cat said. He shrugged.

"OK, I will," said Emily.

Traitor! Ailsa held her hand up too, of course. And Amrit, who didn't like to be left out of anything.

With any luck they'd all be bored after that. Or the lesson would end or something. Cat sneaked a look at the clock. Still twenty minutes left. Too long.

Cat realized something then. There was only one way to deal with this. Only one way to get Danny off her back. She would have to *pretend* not to mind. No, she wouldn't actually volunteer to touch the thing, but if she got as close as she could, made every possible effort to look as though she didn't mind, Danny would see that this wasn't something he could get her on.

Professor Bryden was coming towards them with his plastic box full of disease-ridden, pointless bark impersonators, followed closely by Miss Bleakney. At that moment, Cat could willingly have strangled Miss Bleakney with her own over-long hair. Look at her: smiling away as though this was just the most exciting biology lesson in the whole history of biology lessons.

Here he was. Cat craned her neck, pretending to be interested.

Professor Bryden stood between her and Bethan, just behind them. He smelled sickly – old-mannish and unwashed – as he leant between them to put the box on the table. He wore a brown tweedy jacket, with baggy pockets.

He reached his hand towards the box and the smell of his jacket caught in her throat. He really was a horrible little man. There was something definitely creepy about him. She was sure he'd looked at her when he'd been walking towards them. Did he sense her fear?

"They're quite cute," she said lightly, as he brought one out and placed it on the back of his hand and she tried not to shrink from him. They weren't cute, not even a little bit. They were disgusting. They looked artificial. Their only skill was in looking like a piece of rotten bark. They couldn't fly, or build webs, or migrate to South Africa, or do anything vaguely clever.

"Well?" said Professor Bryden to Emily. "Are you ready?"

Emily nodded, her face a mixture of excitement and fear. She looked like someone who has just chosen to skydive and is regretting it but going to do it anyway.

"Hold out your hands. Nice and steady." And the whole class watched while Emily did.

Cat struggled to stay in control, to stop her eyes and head buzzing with dizziness. She didn't think she could speak. The thing was so close. And about six centimetres long. It raised its shell a little, and it was all she could do not to gasp. Professor Bryden put a small piece of apple a little way in front of its mouth and it began to walk slowly across Emily's hand towards it.

Emily squealed, "Euuch, it's tickling! It's horrible!"

It was indeed horrible. How on earth could anyone find it anything other than horrible? It was disgusting and also incredibly boring. Cat felt trapped by both the disgustingness and the boringness of this thing. She made a vow there and then to give up biology at the very earliest opportunity. What was the point in devoting precious hours to studying such a stupid subject?

The world was extremely badly designed sometimes.

Presumably her parents had both had to study insects since they must both have done biology. But what was the point even for them? Did any one single thing about cockroaches come into their work? Mind you, madness and insects couldn't be that far apart. She thought of Danny and his collection. Probably he'd end up as one of her mother's patients.

"OK, my turn," said Ailsa, way too keen for Cat's liking.

"It's cute," lied Cat, fixing a smile on her face with a huge effort. "I like its kind of shiny shell."

"And no wings, you note," said Professor Bryden.

Surely this was nearly over now?

Over Professor Bryden's shoulder, Cat could see Danny. Smiling at her. Grinning. He mouthed something at her. One word. Nothing particularly bad. But enough.

Loser.

She could not let that go.

CHAPTER 12
DEATH

CAT'S mouth was dry and she felt the beginning of true panic. She wished she could be somewhere else. Anywhere. Everyone was looking at her, waiting for her. She had no choice. Well, she could scream and leave the room, but she'd never live it down.

"OK," she said. "No big deal. I'll hold it. After you, Ailsa."

"No, go on, you go first," said Ailsa. Grinning. Probably just a game to her — nothing malicious — but Ailsa didn't know how hard this was. That it was serious; that Cat's skin was crawling at the thought of touching this creature.

There was no point in postponing it — it was like jumping into cold water: you just had to do it without thinking too much.

It required every effort to force her hands out in front of her. Emily began to move her hands towards

Cat, to pass the thing over. Slowly. No problem. Well, yes, a problem, but not an impossible one.

What happened next? When Cat thought about it afterwards, she couldn't quite decide. It was as though someone jogged Ailsa and she in turn knocked the box with the other cockroaches, which Professor Bryden had put on the table; and at exactly the same time, just as Cat's eyes were drawn suddenly to the box, she saw that two insects had half crawled out of it. Some of the other pupils must have seen this at the same time, because a couple of them shrieked. Emily's hands came quickly towards Cat, opening as she tried to drop her cargo as fast as possible, but Cat wasn't ready. She panicked.

Unable to stop herself, she flung her arm out in self-defence. It was a reflex action, something Miss Bleakney had told them about, designed to save you from a deadly enemy.

So Cat's hand hit the insect with the power of a squash racquet. Emily squealed and pushed her seat back. The insect ricocheted violently off the hard table and flew with huge force onto the floor. People screamed. Cat couldn't see the creature as she was on the other side of the table, but from the sound everyone was making, it was injured. She thought cockroaches were meant to be indestructible. Professor Bryden had already been going on about that.

"Ergh, that's horrible!" said Alison.

"Do something!" said Bethan.

"Aw, the poor wee thing. Help it someone!"

Professor Bryden rushed round to that side, with a kind of strangled moan. He looked at it. Cat moved so she too could see it. The creature limped away, some of its legs damaged, lopsided now, leaning like a broken toy. Cat felt sick. But it wasn't her fault — she hadn't asked to hold the thing.

"Someone pass my bag," ordered Professor Bryden, his voice tight.

Miss Bleakney hurried to fetch it. Otherwise she was no use at all. She flapped about, trying to get the pupils back to their seats. But she had little success, since this was about the most interesting thing that had happened in a biology lesson since The Explosion, an incident that did not appear in the school prospectus.

With pain on his face, Professor Bryden opened his bag, his movements quick and fluid. He seemed to be making soothing noises towards the creature. He took a brown bottle from his bag. And a glass jar with something white at the bottom.

"Stand back!" he ordered. And when no one did, he raised his voice, shrill now. "Stand back, I said!"

He knelt down beside the patient. Pulled thin rubber gloves onto his hands, flexing his fingers. Tried to open the glass jar. But the lid was too tight and his hands were old-looking, slightly twisted and knobbly as though with arthritis.

"I'll do it, Sir," said Marcus.

"No, you won't. Thank you," muttered the man. Grimacing with effort, he eventually managed to get the lid off and he then opened the brown bottle. In the lid was a dropper. "Stand back further!" he ordered. Holding it as far as he could from his face, he squeezed the dropper, gathering up some of the liquid in the bottle. He began to drip the clear fluid into the glass jar, where it landed on the hard white substance at the bottom. Carefully, he replaced the lid on the bottle, but not before one drop had landed on the floor. Without fuss, he wiped it with his gloved finger.

"Stand back!" shouted Miss Bleakney now, as if she realized that this could be a dangerous chemical.

Quickly, but gently, he lifted the struggling insect. It hissed viciously as he lowered it into the jar and finally screwed the lid on. In another swift movement, he peeled the gloves from his hands and put them in the hazardous waste container that Miss Bleakney held out for him.

The insect became still. The man put the jar away in his bag, along with the brown bottle.

"Back to your seats everyone," said Miss Bleakney. She was tight-lipped.

As for Professor Bryden, he looked furious. He was no longer just a silly little man with a shiny head. His eyes were venomous as he looked around the faces: faces that all looked at him.

Silent faces. Of pupils who did not know what to say or think. A strange tension settled on them, a trapped energy, excitement mixed with horror. Cat felt exposed, guilty, yet angry too.

"That should never have happened," said Professor Bryden, his voice menacing. "That insect need not have died, not at all. Why you need to be frightened of a tiny insect, I simply have no idea. Clearly it had more cause to be frightened of you. And yet it was not. How does that make you feel?" He looked around. Cat was sure he looked mostly at her.

"Quite," said Miss Bleakney. "But they are only young. Perhaps we…" She stopped. "Now, everyone, I think we should thank Professor Bryden very much for coming in and sharing his knowledge with us." And she started vigorous clapping. The noise of applause rose strangely into the room, shattering the tension, and now scattered laughter broke out. Miss Bleakney shouted above the noise.

"Quiet, please! Quiet! Marcus, please go to 4M and tell them that they may not come to the lab until I say so. And Rebecca, please go and get one of the cleaners – tell them there's been a chemical spillage. Quickly, please. No, don't be silly, Josh, we're not all doomed. It's just a precaution." She ushered them out of the room as fast as possible.

This incident quickly spread around the school. Opinion was divided. For some, the man was a creep and should never have brought live insects into the class. But on several occasions during the morning break, pupils in the year below called Cat a murderer. Why her? Why not whoever had jogged Ailsa, or Emily who'd thrown the creature towards her when she wasn't ready?

Cat's friends stuck up for her. The others who'd been in the class didn't care much whose fault it was. After all, it had been an exciting lesson and something to talk about. And it was only an insect. Danny? He grinned and looked her way at every opportunity. He was thoroughly enjoying himself.

Cat just wanted the day to end.

"Don't worry. They'll soon forget about it," said Marcus. Marcus was sensible like that. And Cat knew he was right. Bethan and Ailsa stayed with her all through school, and she was glad of their loyalty, even though Bethan was somewhat exaggerating the drama of the situation. And Emily had said sorry, though it wasn't her fault either – Cat knew she would have done just the same.

Then, of course, there were the rumours. Rebecca said she'd seen Professor Bryden coming out of the head's office, looking furious. One rumour said he was crying. Alison was sure she'd seen him wiping his eyes. When a police car was seen in the school grounds, he'd *obviously* been arrested. When no one could be sure that they'd seen him *in* the car, he'd *obviously* escaped and was now on the run, a dangerous criminal. No matter that the school secretary laughed and said that the police had only been there because they were doing a talk to the juniors: that was *obviously* a cover-up. One rumour said that Miss Bleakney was going to be sacked. She'd been seen coming out of the head's office too. By the end of the day, Professor Bryden was definitely a paedophile with a criminal record, and a murderer too, a poisoner.

Then there was a rumour that the chemical was chloroform. It put you to sleep, everyone said. It was dangerous. The rumours said it was banned by the government and they might all get cancer. The school should be evacuated.

Isabel even said she felt sick. Mind you, Isabel often felt sick. It got her out of all sorts of things. She was weedy. Fragile. Needed, frankly, to get a life. But then Bethan said she'd felt sick too. When she thought about it, so had Cat, but she didn't think it was the chemical.

Cat couldn't shake the incident from her mind. Her skin crawled when she thought of it.

At the end of school, instead of going home with the others as usual, she made some excuse, something about going back to fetch a book. Instead, she went to the biology lab. Knocked on the door.

"Come in." Miss Bleakney was there, packing her books into a bag. She looked up when Cat came in.

"What can I do for you, Catriona?" Her voice had a touch of frost. She looked tired, too, her make-up almost all dissolved into the sweat of the day.

"I came to say I'm sorry about what happened," said Cat. "I couldn't help it. I really hate insects and I thought it was going to land on me when…"

Infuriatingly, Cat felt tears pricking behind her eyes. How stupid! But it had been a hard day. Everything going wrong. And the weekend too. Phiz and the athletics stuff. Life running away from her. Suddenly, she felt weighed down, emotional. With a deep breath, she forced it away.

Miss Bleakney smiled at her, though somewhat weakly. "It wasn't your fault, Catriona. I take responsibility. Professor Bryden is not used to talking in schools. He should not have had … well, I should have stepped in earlier. I'm just relieved no one… Anyway, no harm done, eh? Now don't be upset, and don't think any more of it. Off you go."

And Cat did, at least partly relieved.

She would put it from her mind.

It was only an insect. Really no big deal. No harm could come from its death.

CHAPTER 13
HUMILIATION

BACK in his home, he fumes and shakes, unable to keep still. He had almost been knocked down while riding home on his bicycle, so preoccupied had he been. So angry, so ashamed.

It is all that girl's fault. Stupid little fool. With her pretty eyes and big hair and make-up. What was she doing in a biology lesson with her hair all dangerously loose round her face like that? Didn't schools have rules any more?

Pathetic, she was, with her fear of his insects. A huge human with clodhopping feet, who could kill an insect with one swat – and actually had, come to think of it, or more or less. Injured it anyway. He'd only asked her to hold it, for goodness' sake. In fact, he'd only been trying to help her. He'd seen the fear on her face. He'd thought how good it would be if he could cure her fear. And when he'd tried to, it had all gone wrong.

And the ethyl acetate. How could they criticize him for using it? They didn't know anything about it. It wasn't even particularly dangerous to humans or not in those small quantities. He is one of the most experienced scientists ever likely to set foot in that school, accustomed to working with such a chemical; has used it all his working life; has a licence for it, for crying out loud!

Well, had a licence. Yes, it was technically out of date, but does that really matter? He is an eminent scientist. Yes, retired, but once a scientist always a scientist. You don't lose all your knowledge just because you retire through ill health.

He paces up and down the room. Panic is beginning to rise in his chest. Breathe, breathe, breathe. That's what his doctor said all those years ago. Breathe slowly and the feelings of panic will go away.

But he is so angry. Justifiably. He'd had to sit in that head teacher's office and watch her as she told him that the incident was unfortunate and that her first concern was her pupils' safety. She appreciated, she'd said, that he was not acquainted with the modern rules of engagement with children, and she felt a degree of responsibility, she'd added, and regretted that the biology teacher had not asked him for an Enhanced Disclosure and certain assurances before his visit.

"Enhanced Disclosure?" he'd asked.

"Yes, CRB Disclosure, you may have heard it called. You know..."

"CRB?" he'd asked, none the wiser.

"Criminal Records Bureau. It's—"

"Criminal! What on earth do you mean by *criminal*? I am no criminal!" He had spat the words at her, blazing, bitter fury boiling inside.

"No, no, no, of course," she'd replied hurriedly. "It doesn't imply that at all – really it doesn't. It's a legal part of the procedure for making sure that all adults who come in contact with our pupils are appropriate. It's very—"

"Do you think I am *not* appropriate? Do you think I wished them any harm? I tried to educate them, and you stand there accusing me of..."

"You brought a dangerous chemical into the class," she'd said, frostily. "Subject to restricted use. Not for use within a school classroom, with no appropriate procedures being followed."

"Appropriate procedures? I am an expert! I know perfectly well how to handle chemicals. None of your pupils was in any danger at any time. It's one of the safest chemicals for use in the circumstances."

"I am very sorry. I appreciate that you have given up your time, and that you meant no harm. But I am sure you will understand—"

"No, I do not. I was trying to educate your pupils, to break down the barriers of their ignorance. Those girls were ridiculous with their fear and that one girl in particular. Of a tiny insect? What have you been teaching them?"

The woman had bristled, though her voice remained steely cold. "I will not have you insult our pupils or the education we provide for them."

But he would not stop. "I only asked the silly child to hold it. And she agreed; I did not force her. I thought I could cure her fear."

"There are procedures. You must—"

And now he'd interrupted her. "Besides, if I wished to, I could very easily complain about the fact that many of your pupils had their hair loose in a science laboratory. What sort of 'procedures' are these? In my day ... oh, what is the use of this? I am leaving now and I do not wish ever to set foot in such a place of ignorance again."

Now he can barely remember how he'd left the room, presumably picking up his bags. It had been shaming. He had felt sweat dripping down his back.

The museum had been informed. By phone. Immediately. He remembers the woman saying that she would have to do this because a dangerous substance had been brought into school and if she didn't alert the authorities and his employer, she would be guilty of a "dereliction of duty". And she had looked at him meaningfully over her narrow spectacles as he left.

Dereliction of duty! How dare she! How dare the woman!

He will not be allowed to talk in a school again – well, do they really think he wants to? But the shame of being told that he may not! The implications!

There'll be a form somewhere: he can imagine it. A record by his name. "Not suitable for working with children." As though he were a paedophile!

His armpits are wet. He can smell himself. And his heart will not stop racing. At this rate, he'll be ill again.

What had he done wrong? The lesson had been going well. He had seen the interest in their eyes. He'd been thinking how well he was doing. He'd even been thinking that perhaps children weren't so objectionable after all, if you got them on their own territory. Maybe kids were just like insects: you needed to know how to handle them. He'd often been called the insect whisperer; on field trips he'd seemed to know exactly where to find each species. So maybe you just had to learn to be a child whisperer.

He'd been reluctant to take on this task in the first place; he'd never done a talk in a school before.

"You'll enjoy it," Miss Logan, the education officer at the museum, had said.

Well, what did she know? She hadn't had a clue whether he'd enjoy it – she'd just been saying that because she'd had to find someone for the task.

And he'd been it.

Well, he was the person for the task. In theory.

It was that girl's fault. Silly, pathetic, spoilt kid. Did she ever think about others? If she only knew where her stupidity had got him. How it has ruined him, perhaps.

How can he go back to work at the museum now?

He feels palpitations, chest pains, an overwhelming blackness coming over him. His eyes prick with tears. His life is all falling to pieces again. Just as it did when he had to give up work through nervous exhaustion. It was panic attacks then, too.

It must not happen! He must do something. He must take back control.

Somehow.

CHAPTER 14
SINISTER HAPPENINGS

A dark dry wind whipped the early leaves off the ground as Cat set off for the swimming pool on Tuesday evening the following week. Car headlights shone on the main road ahead.

She looked to the left as she closed the door. A cyclist was coming round the corner, no helmet, his body bulky in a coat. He did not look at her as he sped past and soon turned right onto the main road.

She took a deep breath. She really didn't feel like training today. But she still hadn't found the moment to say anything to her parents. It wasn't easy. And, hanging there in her mind, was the knowledge of her grandfather, and that her mum kind of thought she'd follow in his footsteps. Every now and then she'd say how proud he'd be of Cat. But he was an old man who'd lived in another time, another world. He couldn't begin to understand her if he were alive today.

He'd never known her and she'd never known him.

And her friends might drift away if she didn't spend enough time with them. Bethan was starting to go out with Josh. All the pairings and friendships were changing – what if she wasn't around to be part of it?

Sport had always made her feel secure, something she knew she did well. But maybe it was also a trap and she'd get stuck in it, left behind by the rest of life.

She had to tell her parents. Get out of the trap. As soon as possible.

Cat pressed her headphones into her ears and selected the music she wanted. She turned right onto the main road and began to walk.

She buried herself in the music as she walked, speeding up, getting her heart rate going. The walk or jog to the fitness centre was a good warm-up. She would start running in a moment. She adjusted the bag on her back, made sure it was properly fastened. Checked that her phone was there.

The wind blew into her eyes, carrying leaves and dust with it. It was oddly warm, like a desert wind. Cat quickened her pace and rounded the corner. Two men stood some metres ahead, under a streetlight, one holding the other by the arm, as though about to lead him across the road. The one being held was looking at her as she came round the corner. She saw that he was staring straight at her, wide-eyed. Cat tried not to look at him, but she'd seen his face before she could look away: the mouth open, the cheeks hollowed in the orange light, the hair hanging straggly and greasy from under a knitted hat. A young man.

He was shaking his head from side to side. The other man gripped his shoulders, calming him.

She hurried on. She wanted to go the other way, but she was committed to this direction. The man shouted – crazy nonsense. Some kind of mental patient, probably a day patient from the hospital. Out with his friend, or maybe his carer. The carer spoke to him firmly, trying to make him look away from her.

The man waved his arms wildly in Cat's direction. Most of his words were unintelligible to her, but some were clear enough. Even over the sound of her iPod. She caught the words, "She's bad! Bad!" amid the nonsense. He was trying to get away, trying to cross the road into the traffic. The carer was holding him back.

As she came level with the men, she looked towards them, forced a quick smile and a muttered hello before hurrying on. She only wanted to reassure them. But the young man just shouted more loudly. "Bad! Bad!"

As soon as she could, Cat began to jog. If her friends had been with her they could all have laughed about it together. An odd hysteria rose inside her.

But, although the young man was clearly seriously unstable, it still left a horrible feeling. What kind of illness did he have? Could it be schizophrenia? She knew that usually involved hearing voices, seeing things that weren't there. What had he seen when he looked at her? Why did he look at her with such fear and horror? She shivered.

She hoped that carer knew what he was doing.

How could her mum work with people like that? How frightening to face it every day. She hoped her mum would always have someone with her when she had to see patients like him. Probably there were rules to protect her, safety procedures or whatever.

Cat jogged on and tried to put the incident from her.

A little more than ten minutes later, she was at the fitness centre. She breathed in the warm, heavy smell of chlorine. This was where she felt in control, safe. This was what she loved: the feeling of wellbeing that came over her like a drug when she exercised.

Her grandfather must have known this feeling. Maybe he even had the same conflicts as she did. What did he feel like when he had to give up through injury? But what he'd *felt* had never been part of the story told about him. Maybe no one knew or thought about it. He was spoken of like some soldier killed in a war – heroic and dead. But not real.

She lowered herself into the comfortable water and pushed off, slipping into an easy freestyle. She had a lane to herself and she was able to switch her mind off, concentrating solely on her muscles, her breathing, the rhythm, feeling her own strength.

There were three other swimmers: a woman and two men. All swimming seriously, ploughing up and down the lanes. But she was as good as any of them, slicing through the water as if it were her natural habitat. One by one, they all stopped swimming and left the pool. She was on her own in the soft, warm water.

Cat swam on. She ignored everything apart from herself and the water. She ignored the silently spinning exercise bikes in the gym through the toughened glass. She ignored the lifeguard, an old guy, sitting on his high perch. And, after a brief flash of irritation, she ignored the one man watching from the gallery. If you concentrate hard enough you can ignore anything – it's something you learn to do when you're an athlete. Ignore bad feelings, ignore unwanted attention and comments, ignore everything except speed, strength, technique and winning.

She put the bad feelings of the last few days behind her: the lousy weekend, the incident with the insect, her parents' moods, Danny, the creep on Phiz. That, incidentally, seemed to have ended: when she'd gone online the last few times, nothing had happened. Oh, apart from her laptop behaving badly, being slow to load and crashing once when she was in the middle of something. But the guy with the spider had gone.

She would do some extra lengths. It was a mental thing, winning – you had to have winning in your mind. That's what her coach was always saying. And he was right. It was amazing the difference in performance if you thought you were a winner.

And Cat *was* a winner. No one would take that away from her. Certainly not a jerk like Danny.

Cat was ready to leave the fitness centre an hour

and a half later, tingling with energy, her body not even slightly tired after twenty extra lengths. She took her phone out of her bag as she stood just inside the entrance. Phoned home. As promised.

Her mum answered. "Hello, Catty. Sorry, Dad's not home yet. He'll be here any minute. No, wait; I'll phone him and tell him to pick you up. Just stay there. Inside the centre. I'll keep you posted."

"Can't you come and get me?"

"I'm really sorry – I had a glass of wine. Anja came round. I thought Dad would be back in time. Can you just wait? Maybe ten minutes. Less even."

"All right. But I'll phone Dad and if he's not nearly here I'll walk."

"No, Catty. You won't."

"I'll run then. I'll be fine." Though she remembered the power cut. The feeling of being chased.

It wouldn't happen again. The only reason she was even thinking about it was that it was the same time, same place.

"No, Catty. It's too dark. Do as you're told and stay there. If necessary I'll come and get you in a taxi."

"But, Mum, I've got homework to do! I *need* to get home."

"Just be patient. Anyway, if you don't get off the phone, I can't phone Dad. See you soon."

Cat fumed. All because her mum's friend come round and wine had simply *had* to be consumed. Sometimes, parents just didn't think ahead.

She sat on one of the moulded plastic benches inside the reception area, fiddling with her phone. The hard-faced receptionist was flicking through a magazine, looking bored. Cat stared out into the darkness, willing her dad to arrive quickly. The fitness centre was on a wide but quiet road, a residential district. On the other side of it, she could see the dark area where the park was. Which she'd have to cross to get to the main road to pick up a bus or taxi. Or to run home. As she wanted to.

Why couldn't she do that? So much easier.

When would her mum phone? Cat should have insisted she'd phone him herself. But her mum always had to take over.

The occasional car went past.

A thin figure stood hunched under some trees over there, collar up.

Footsteps behind her. She swung round.

CHAPTER 15
SIRENS

A man had come from the changing rooms. His hair was wet. He put his bag on the bench beside Cat and spent some time putting his things away and zipping the bag up.

"You're a good swimmer. Powerful."

"Thanks." She wished he would go away. She was not used to strange men talking to her and it made her feel uncomfortable. On the other hand, no one actually dislikes praise.

A thought hit her with a small punch: he was the man who had been watching from the gallery.

Cat sneaked a look at the man, just a glance. His face was turned slightly away but she could see his profile. Tough, no flab, thick muscled neck. Very short, lightish brown hair. A hard man, into fitness by the look of him. But not particularly creepy. Ordinary clothes, no dirty raincoat. A sort of bulky, padded coat that he was just pulling on now.

A glance towards the receptionist showed her still reading her magazine, not noticing anything else. Nothing could happen while she was there.

Cat didn't look at him any more. Even when he spoke to her.

"You swim for a club? You should."

"I do." She wouldn't, of course, tell him which one. She knew all about not talking to strangers. Had done it in nursery.

Then she realized that she didn't need to tell him: her tracksuit and her bag both had the club's name emblazoned onto them. A chill scurried through her.

But what harm could come of it? He couldn't know where she lived, or her name, or anything. Anyway, she was being paranoid. She was becoming as bad as her parents.

Whatever, she wished he would go.

Her phone rang. Dad. "Catriona – Mum says you're waiting at the fitness centre? I'll be there in five minutes, OK? Look out for me from inside the entrance."

"OK, Dad. Thanks." She kept the phone conspicuously in her hand and said *Dad* particularly clearly for the benefit of the man. But when she looked round, he had gone.

She looked through the doors again. It had begun to rain suddenly, veiling the trees, turning everything into a darker shade of shadow. A cyclist left from the car park of the fitness centre – probably the man who had spoken to her, judging by the shape of the coat. The figure under the trees had gone, too.

The sound of sirens swelled in the distance. Many sirens. Police, fire or ambulance – she couldn't tell which. A few seconds later she saw the lights go past on the main road on the other side of the park: flashing blue lights, urgent, blaring. A few seconds later, more vehicles passed. Gradually the sound faded into the distance.

Something big. A major fire maybe. But nothing that needed to concern her.

Mind you, her parents, being cynical, were boring on the subject of sirens. "That'll be them wanting to get home for their tea," they would say, knowingly. How did they know? What if someone was dying? What if someone actually died while her parents were accusing the emergency services of rushing home to tea?

Adults took the wrong things seriously. Worrying about things like Phiz and *not* worrying about fire engines, police and ambulances trying to prevent deaths.

Anyway, there was her dad. The car was pulling up, the window easing down.

"In you get! Quickly!"

"What's the hurry?"

"It's raining, in case you hadn't noticed."

"Yes, but I'm the one getting wet," she said as she clambered in.

"Yes, well, I've got a lot to do this evening. I've had to come out of my way. And the traffic's appalling. Something's happened."

"I heard loads of sirens."

"There's something going on near the bridges: Chambers Street, apparently. The buses have been rerouted. Everything's blocked off."

"What sort of thing?"

"No idea. Probably a fire. Could be lots of things. An old tenement that they've decided isn't safe. Someone threatening to jump off a building. Who knows? Could be nothing."

Later that evening, they heard what it was. Someone had phoned the police to say there was a bomb at the museum. Nothing had been found. So far. Could be a hoax. But the threat was being taken seriously.

Who would do such a thing? Why the museum? Surely it wasn't a terrorist target.

Cat thought nothing of it, other than to feel that familiar fear that she felt whenever she thought of terrorists. When wars were in other countries, they were horrible, but far away. They made her feel bad inside, scared, sad, but they didn't affect her life. The threat of terrorism felt like something against her, her future. She needed not to think about it. She needed her life to stay safe. How did people manage to cope with danger in their lives every day? She couldn't imagine what it must be like to feel unsafe when you went out of your front door. Did you get used to it? Or did it eat you up?

Her dad was swearing now. A motorbike was driving too close behind them. He pulled over to the left very suddenly and for a moment it seemed as though the motorbike would pull over too, but at the last minute it sped past, the leather-jacketed rider peering round at them and glaring.

"What's his problem?" muttered her dad. "Maniac!"

"I think it was a woman, actually," Cat said.

"Maniac, anyway."

Once home, Cat went to the kitchen for a snack, took it upstairs, and had a shower. She came out feeling better, clean, warm, comfortable. While she waited for her hair to dry, she went on Phiz. Just planning to chat with her friends while she ate her snack, before doing her homework.

It didn't happen like that.

When she clicked the Phiz icon to launch it, the screen started to behave oddly. The background seemed to quiver, as though breaking up into millions of pieces.

Phiz took ages to launch. Irritating. Maybe she needed her laptop repaired. Perhaps she could get someone to take a look at it at school. Marcus was good with computers – maybe he could sort it out. Danny could have done as well, but how likely was she to ask him?

Eventually the Phiz screen launched. And slowly came into focus.

A small, hollow groan escaped her lips.

The whole screen was full of flies, crawling everywhere. Thousands, millions maybe. A distant buzzing came from the computer. She turned the sound back up a little, and quickly turned it down – she'd hoped it might just be the sound of the speakers, but it wasn't. Even with the sound turned down, she could faintly hear the noise.

The flies began to shrink, and to swarm quickly towards the top-right corner. There, they poured into a small black hole and disappeared. And when they had gone, Cat could see what the small black hole actually was.

A spider with an open mouth. The spider was back.

CHAPTER 16
INSECTS WATCHING

HORROR crawled through Cat's body. She could not take her eyes from the screen. She slid the laptop from her, slowly, touching it with only the tips of her fingers. Her breathing quickened, raced. Something stuck in her throat. Nothing around her seemed to exist except for this screen and the buzzing.

Footsteps on the stairs.

"Catty?" Her mum.

"Yes?"

"Can I come in?"

"Why?" she snapped.

"To say good night. Ask you about your day. Is that a problem?"

"No. Goodnight." Cat closed the lid of the laptop.

Her mum came further in. "What's wrong? You look awful."

"Thanks a lot. I'm just tired." She knew her voice

sounded tight. She couldn't help it.

"Don't snap, sweetheart. I'm only asking. Anything wrong at school?"

"No. Nothing."

"You sure? Swimming go OK? You up with your schedule?"

"Fine."

"I'm sorry Dad and I have been a bit preoccupied the last few days. It's sorted now – you know that Gulf War syndrome article? Well, it's fine. A journalist phoned twice, but I gave him nothing and he won't bother me again. Nothing to worry about."

"I know."

"Are you sure you're OK? You look really stressed. Has something happened?"

"Stop going *on*, Mum, OK? I'm just tired. I'm going to bed now." Her voice was snappier than she wanted, but she couldn't stop it.

"OK, sweetheart. Just tell me if there's anything I can do, OK?" And her mum came, kissed the top of her head and left. Cat did not move towards her, though a moment later she wished she had. The scent of her was so familiar, so warm. She felt a sudden need to bury her head in her mum's shoulder, as she used to do. Not to have secrets. To tell her mum everything, because her mum always used to make everything all right. But the words would not come. Because everything now seemed complicated and tangled in dangerous truths.

If she gave any hint that something was wrong,

everything would pour out.

Besides, this started with Phiz. It was her fault, they'd say. Her parents had forbidden her to have an account. She'd probably wrecked her laptop and it could cost a fortune to sort it. She could not tell them. And she'd have to talk about Danny and that was off-limits with parents. They wouldn't take it seriously. Or they'd take it too seriously.

Her mum was gone.

She opened the laptop again. She needed to talk to Bethan or Ailsa. Or Marcus, to ask if he could help with the laptop.

She went onto another site to talk to them; see who was there.

They were not online. None of her close friends was there. And there wasn't enough credit on her phone to speak to them: there never was.

She was on her own.

Cat slept badly again that night. Every time she closed her eyes she saw that spider, heard the flies buzzing. Every time she opened her eyes she saw darkness.

At one point she got out of bed to open her shutters and lighten the blackness of her room. Outside, grey moonlight shone through a sky patched with clouds. A glow came from the sallow orange streetlights.

Something moved in the undergrowth of the garden opposite the house, a back garden of a house in the next street. A fox, maybe. There were lots of foxes around here. Polly regarded it as her night-time duty to follow their smells on her bedtime walk.

Through the branches of the surrounding trees, Cat could see the lights of windows. Many leaves still remained, though each windy day shook more away. Soon she would be able to see more windows. Now it was only the highest ones and some in the distance. Cat was not worried about people looking into her window; she was high enough to look down on most of them. And the others? Well, she wouldn't have her curtains open if her light was on, obviously. But if her light was off, no one could see her: her dad had explained it years ago when she'd been about six and worried about it. He'd done an experiment to prove it. It gave her a good feeling. Of being invisible.

She gave no thought to who might be behind the lit windows. The fact that she couldn't sleep; the fact that she had stupidly let a virus into her computer and might get into trouble, or lose the work on it – her coursework maybe; the fact that she had creep Danny plaguing her; the fact that tomorrow was fencing again: these were the things that mattered.

Not who might or might not be behind those windows. Watching.

CHAPTER 17
THE SECOND DUEL

CAT grabbed hold of Marcus as soon as she saw him the following morning. At the school gates. Stamping her feet in the cold of a late September sun. She'd been waiting. Bethan had arrived first and Cat had told her half the story when Marcus turned up. With Ailsa. Walking quite close together. Anyway, she started to tell him about the laptop as they all walked towards the classroom. Josh had joined them, tagging on to Bethan, the two of them messing around together. Cat ignored them.

"You've got to help me, Marcus. And I don't want everyone to know about this. You've got to promise." He nodded. And they all started listening – a secret was always worth attention. Cat told them what had happened with her laptop.

"How could Danny be such a creep?" asked Ailsa. "What a total loser!"

"I didn't even know he was that clever," said Bethan.

"Actually, you don't need to be that clever. There're sites that sell small viruses, bits of code you can upload to someone's computer if they give you access. He could have bought one." Marcus was in his element, his eyes thoughtful beneath his dark floppy hair.

"I don't believe it was Danny," said Josh. "He's not like that. He can be an idiot but he wouldn't do something like that. That's sick."

"He would," said Bethan. "Where Cat's concerned he's lost the plot."

"But it's OK," said Ailsa. "It's easy to get rid of a virus."

They looked at her. "My dad does this stuff," she said. "He had to deal with my computer in the holidays because I'd got a virus and he said it had come from Phiz. That's why I got banned." Cat remembered that Ailsa's dad worked in computers. "Anyway, it's quite interesting, actually."

"You got banned?" asked Marcus. "But you were on yesterday." Oh, so, not when Cat wanted to speak to them, then.

"Yeah, I got banned. But so what? They're not going to watch me every minute, are they?"

"But can you get rid of it without my parents knowing?" asked Cat. "They're going to kill me if I've wrecked my laptop."

"Easy," said Marcus, and Ailsa nodded. "At the very worst, I'll take it back to factory settings," he said. "Have you got the recovery disk?"

"I haven't a clue. What's that?"

"Your mum or dad will have it," said Ailsa. "You'll just have to find where." Cat knew where it'd be: her mum was organized like that, had everything to do with various electronic stuff in a box. Everything labelled. It wouldn't be a problem.

"Have you backed up your stuff?" asked Marcus.

"What do *you* think?"

Of course she hadn't. Not recently anyway. They'd been warned about it at the start of the school year. All about taking responsibility now that they were working for serious exams. But Cat hadn't taken much notice. It had seemed like one of those dire warnings that teachers give, but it's never going to happen. She'd backed up once, the day they'd been warned, but hadn't done it again. She felt slightly sick.

They had to go to registration then. Josh and Bethan, whispering about something. Ailsa and Marcus, discussing computers. And Cat. Ready for a bad day.

Later, she was on the receiving end of a row from Mr Dawson about not having her homework from last night. Well, OK, not last night. Yes, she should have done it over the weekend ... yes, she knew she'd had a whole week to do it ... yes, she knew she shouldn't have left it till the last minute ... sorry, Sir ... thank you, Sir. The thank you was because he said he'd let her off but, he added, "Only if I have it by tomorrow. Without fail."

Which she'd had to accept. Though even if Marcus

and Ailsa between them were able to fix her laptop, the chances of her being able to get the work done in time were minimal. But that was a row to deal with when it came. Better tomorrow than today.

She'd also face hassle tomorrow if the two bits of work she had already started for other teachers ended up disappearing into the great graveyard of homework in the sky.

Gloom settled on her. It was a day when everything was going to go wrong.

The day dragged its way through double English and religious moral education in the morning; dragged its way through lunch of a huge grey baked potato with the choice of fillings being cheese or not cheese, and a salad of wet tomatoes and lettuce with beige edges; and finally dragged its way through French and maths, ending with another row for forgetting her calculator.

The only good thing was that since Danny wasn't in her set for maths, French or English, she barely saw him.

Until fencing.

Bethan, Marcus and Josh had gone to drama, with Marcus promising to come to her house later on to deal with the virus. Emily was at cookery. Ailsa normally did fencing but she had to go to the dentist. Priya was off sick. Cat was on her own.

She was aware of Danny as they prepared for the class in the school gym. Both in their protective kit already, they each selected foils and masks, along with everyone else. Danny's left hand had a small bandage on two of the fingers.

Cat wanted to cool the situation. She didn't like confrontation, though she wouldn't run away from it if it came. But she wasn't about to make it worse. So she looked at Danny casually, even slightly smiled. He looked away. Whether he'd seen her and deliberately looked away, or just happened to be looking away anyway, she couldn't tell.

She avoided being paired against him. Made sure she was already partnered with someone whenever Mr Boyd was allocating opponents. She worked hard too, trying to please Mr Boyd, concentrating on what she did well: anything to do with sport.

She felt the strength in her thigh muscles as she lunged and parried, focused on the correct position of every part of her body. She listened carefully when Boyd taught them a new move. Did everything she was told. But praise never came. He didn't seem to notice her. When she executed a new move perfectly in one practice bout, he wasn't even looking in her direction.

Sometimes you want to be invisible. Sometimes you don't.

At the end of the lesson she pulled off the sweaty mask and shook her hair free.

Frustrated.

Right, she would deal with this. She walked over to Danny. Spoke to him quietly. This wasn't something for everyone to know about.

"Let's call it quits, shall we?"

"What are you talking about?" He spoke loudly. One of his friends turned towards them.

"You know. Phiz. All that stuff. I'm sorry, OK? Now can we just move on?"

"I don't know what you're talking about. What about Phiz?" Was that knowledge in his eyes?

"Forget it, Danny." And she walked away, her jaw tight with irritation. It had been stupid. She was no closer to any kind of resolution. No closer to knowing if he'd really done it.

Of course he had. But Marcus was going to get rid of the virus thing and after that she could just forget about it. Maybe one day Danny would grow up and it would all blow over. She'd been stupid to think she could have made it up with him so quickly.

She hurried home, among the first to leave, not wanting to have to share a bus with Danny. Darkness was falling and a breeze rustled in her ears. On the bus journey, she plugged in her iPod and immersed herself in the music.

Fifteen minutes later, as she turned into her street and approached her house, she could not help thinking of the spider on her laptop. She shuddered. The idea of someone, Danny, paying for a computer virus, just to frighten her with a spider, knowing she hated them, that was seriously sinister.

She stopped dead. How could she not have thought of this before? The flowers — the dead spider! Could

Danny have sent the flowers? And put the spider in? If he could pay for a virus, he could pay for flowers. OK, he'd never bought her flowers when they'd been going out, but then he wasn't a flowers kind of guy and to be honest she wasn't a flowers kind of girl. But he was a spider kind of guy.

If Danny was responsible for Phiz and the flowers, then... Wasn't that stalking or something? But how could she be sure it was him?

Because it couldn't be anyone else, could it?

CHAPTER 18
THE WATCHER AGAIN

TWO WEEKS AHEAD: OCTOBER

THERE is a nasty acid feeling in his brain. He tries to stay calm, but the feeling will not go away. He looks out of the window, between the trees, into the darkness of early evening. He can see the street, the house, the black door.

Why can he not just get on with his project? It was supposed to make him feel better. He has got past the note-reading stage now and is well into the difficult part: finding the words for his memories. Expressing them.

But he had not expected that emotion would get in the way so much, that he would feel unable to control it. He had thought that he would simply be able to do what he set out to do. He had known that writing it all down would bring the past to the surface again but he had thought that it would feel cleansing. It was his ex-wife who had suggested it in the first place, that he should write down everything that had happened all those years ago.

And what did she know? Silly, misguided cow. Soft, sad and wrecked. Probably she should write her own memories down – she had enough of them to deal with. And yes, he still felt guilty about that. He was not a monster, after all. Which was why he still saw her sometimes. Because he did care about her. And they had loved each other once, until life – or death – had got in the way.

Perhaps he shouldn't be writing his memoirs. He could have just carried on as before. He had been doing OK. No mortgage, his comfortable apartment and some money left to him by his parents; his war pension; a small income from his delivery job. No children to drain his finances.

Of course, the memories. And when Sheila had said he should write them down, it had seemed like a good idea. And then living within sight of the McPherson house, that was the constant reminder. The inspiration, almost. The memory trigger.

Seeing them every day, while dredging his mind for memories, that was hard to take. It was hard to stay focused, balanced. And now he also had Sheila to worry about. Her recent behaviour was ... concerning. Ever since August. *Obsessed* would not be too strong a word. And now he was worried what she might do. She was unpredictable, at the very least. Though he had to confess she probably had more reason than many to behave unpredictably.

Worrying about her is not what he needs. He has his own worries, his own past to deal with. But he does care about her, can't help it.

And then he'd come across Diana McPherson's article while researching Gulf War syndrome, so that he would at least have the science at his fingertips. He'd phoned her, pretending to be a journalist. He shouldn't have done that.

But she'd said nothing. "No comment." In that stuck-up, clinical voice. And he'd come from the phone with buttoned fury.

His mind is blankening rapidly, like chalk words being washed away by rain. He needs something to drink. He goes to the kitchen and puts the kettle on. Perhaps the caffeine hit will wake him up. The angry shriek of the coffee grinder gets under his skin. He keeps the button pressed for as long as it needs. Now he inhales the rich bitter smell. Goes through the coffee-making process carefully. For he is always careful in things like this, routine things that keep his mind on track.

Perhaps he needs to go for a walk. Or to cycle?

He feels a chemical rush, a need to act, a grating desire to lash out: the caffeine only strengthening it. He feels his thoughts scatter.

There is only one thing to do to calm himself down. He takes a key to the specially crafted cupboard. The lock turns with a soft, satisfying clunk, and the double doors reveal the shallow drawers with their elegant labels. He pulls open the drawer with his favourite dragonflies. He takes the lids from a few boxes and pauses to choose. Which will he look at? Which will be his pleasure this evening? Will it be the stunning blue and green patterns of *Aeshna cyanea* or the vivid red of *Crocothemis erythraea*?

He cannot choose. He knows them all too well. He needs a new insect for his collection. He will go on the internet to decide which one he will search for.

Topping up his mug of coffee, he sits down in front of his computer, leaving the drawers of his insect cupboard open. But as the internet page spreads across his screen, the doorbell rings. It jangles his head unpleasantly. Who could this be?

He goes to the intercom and snaps, "Yes?"

"It's me."

Damn. He'd forgotten that his nephew was coming round this evening. He'd forgotten to get his favourite biscuits in. Never mind, he must have something suitable in his kitchen for a nearly fifteen-year-old boy, and his nephew could help him choose his next insect. He liked that.

"Come up, Danny."

He smiles. His insect collection would soon have a new addition.

CHAPTER 19
ATHLETICS

SATURDAY morning. Almost the end of September and an autumn chill in the air. Athletics club – training, not a competition this week. Thursday and Friday were best forgotten, thought Cat. On the other hand, Marcus seemed to have got rid of the virus. Without her parents discovering that she'd been on Phiz. She'd found the disks that Ailsa had mentioned and had put them back without problem.

What Marcus did to her laptop had involved her losing all the documents. He had taken it back to this thing he and Ailsa had called "factory settings". Bit like having a new machine, they said. Except that I lose everything on it, she had replied, grimly.

Not that she wasn't grateful. She was extremely grateful, and told them so. With the virus gone, she could make a fresh start. And yes, she'd lost a few bits of work, but she could do them again. All her photos were on Phiz and her music on her iPod, so that hadn't been a problem. And she had her older files on the one back-up disk she'd done after that warning at the start of the year.

So a couple of rows and mild punishments for mislaid work. She'd live. Punishments were nothing more than an irritation. No one died.

She'd been back on Phiz and found her pages. Everything was fine. No spiders. No one watching her. And she wasn't worried about that any more; because she wouldn't be so stupid next time.

Things were looking up. She hadn't particularly wanted to come to training today, but she had. Too difficult to get out of, and since Ailsa was playing in a hockey match and Bethan was baby-sitting for her sister, her friends weren't going to be doing anything without her so she wasn't so bothered.

She decided to run well, please her coach. Here he was now, coming towards her. She finished tightening the laces of her running shoes. Stood up and smiled at him.

Ex-army, he was. And you could kind of tell: something about the bullet-head, the steel eyes, the muscles like iron. A voice that could fire across the stadium with ease. You wouldn't want to be on the wrong side of him.

"Catriona, hope you're ready to put major effort in today? Get those personal bests upped, eh? We need some times to qualify for the next competition."

"Yes, Mr T." she replied.

"Now, I have a whole new training plan to get you started on. You were rubbish the other week. Not even trying, young lady. You need to be pushed to the next level. So I want to work on some specific muscle groups, get you in the gym for an extra hour maybe, and also get some nutritional changes. Your swimming coach wants to up the ante too: build some more muscle…"

"But I don't have *time* for more training." Her heart sank. And she had quite enough muscle already, as far as she was concerned. She didn't want to be some hulking giantess, and that was the trouble with too much swimming.

"Hold on – I'm not talking about more time, not yet. Don't want to overdo it at your age. No, I mean an hour in the gym *instead* of part of your Saturday training. It'll be worth it, I promise. *You're* worth it, Catriona McPherson. You could be the best, you know – and I've said that before but maybe it needs to be said again. You could be one of Scotland's stars. If you tried. *Really* tried."

She used to like it when her coach talked like this. Dreams of distant glory had tasted good. In some ways they still did, but they were definitely losing their sweetness.

On the track, she joined the others in their warm-up activities. She didn't chat to them much. It wasn't easy to. There was an atmosphere. She was the club star, and there was a tinge of jealousy in their attitudes to her.

When the coach singled her out, as he so often did, she could feel the others closing in and shutting her out. She hadn't minded much before: these weren't her friends.

Not being friends with them had made her perform better. It gave her an edge. If they had been friends she might have sometimes held herself back to let them feel better. Probably her coach knew this. She wouldn't be surprised if he even cultivated the edginess between them.

The next half hour passed with Cat focusing on doing exactly what she was told. Praise came often. "Good stuff, Catriona!" he said at the end of each task he chose to set her. Whatever her doubts, as soon as she actually started running, and winning, she revelled in the power and strength it gave her.

Then something happened to throw her concentration away. She was halfway round the track, practising a race strategy for the 1500 metres. She was trying to follow the coach's instructions to the letter, despite the fact that she really wanted to run flat out and lead the field the whole way round.

Out of the corner of her eye, she noticed a figure watching. From the stand, about halfway up. A man, in a heavy coat against the cold. For one strange small moment she was reminded of a film she'd once seen about some Russian spy: he'd stood just like that, in this heavy black coat, collar turned up, binoculars in his hands. People weren't meant to be able to watch training sessions, not without permission, though if someone was using the squash court or something then they could pretty easily find their way to the trackside without being questioned.

Then the man took the binoculars down and pulled a notebook from his pocket. At that point, she realized she'd seen him before. He was the man who'd been watching her at the biathlon competition. She was sure, even at a distance. There was something about his coat and the way he stood.

He lifted the binoculars back to his face.

The coach was striding towards him.

CHAPTER 20
CHIPS

SHE ran faster round the track, ignoring the intended strategy. If he was a rival coach watching her, she would make sure she ran as impressively as possible. Not that she wanted to move to another club, of course, but if she was being watched, she wanted to shine. Purely for the feeling. She passed all the other runners. She was not supposed to be passing them yet, but since the coach wasn't watching it hardly mattered. As long as she looked like a winner to whoever was watching.

The coach was running up the steps. In a few moments, she would have gone round the bend in the track and would no longer be able to see them well. Cat ran faster, now leaving everyone behind. But the man had slipped away.

She ran towards the finishing line, easily beating everyone else. But her coach had barely noticed. He came hurrying towards her now, down the steps. The man had disappeared.

"Who was that?" she asked as her coach came up to her.

"Well run, everyone," he said, tersely. "Catriona, good, good." He obviously hadn't been looking because she knew she hadn't followed instructions.

"But who was it? I think I've seen him before. Maybe."

"Where?"

"At the competition the other week. There was a man watching then. I think it was the same one – same kind of coat anyway."

"Why didn't you say anything?"

The others looked at her, at each other, at their coach. What was going on?

"I don't know. I forgot. I didn't think it was important. Who is he?"

"If you see him again, let me know."

One of the girls spoke. "Is he a pervert or something?"

"Don't be silly, Tessa!"

"How do you know he's not?" asked one of the boys.

"He's probably working for a rival club." He looked at Cat. As though he was about to say something else. But he turned away.

"Right, you lot, round the track again. Connor, Liam, Max, Tessa, get to the blocks and practise sprint starts. Catriona, Rory – to the gym with me. The rest of you, carry on with your programme."

Cat looked back at the stands as she walked towards the gym. The man was still nowhere to be seen.

For the rest of the session, Cat could do nothing wrong. Mr Turner seemed to lavish praise upon her, stayed close to her, gave her all the attention any potential star might need. Well, that was fine. No complaints. And the nutritional stuff – she didn't much like the sound of extra egg white, and she would certainly ignore anything about wholemeal pasta because everyone knew that wholemeal pasta was disgusting, but otherwise it was mostly about eating more of certain things rather than less, and she liked vegetables and fruit anyway, so that was OK. And he didn't *say* anything about not eating chocolate.

As she left the changing-rooms, ready to get the bus home, Mr Turner was there.

"Everything OK, Catriona?" A small frown darkened his forehead.

"Yes, fine, thanks. It was good." Which was true. She felt good. She made as though to go towards the bus stop.

"Getting there, definitely getting there. Don't want to push it too hard though. Not yet. Plenty of time for that. Listen, that man, the one who was watching."

"What?"

"Well, just keep an eye out, OK? I mean, don't speak to him or anything. If he speaks to you, you know the score: don't get into conversation. And tell me."

"Do you think he's from another club?"

"Probably. Or not, I can't be sure. You know there are dodgy people around, whatever I said earlier. You should mention it to your parents and I'll bring it up with the management committee here on Monday. Just to be on the safe side. Procedures and all that. And I'll get the staff to be more vigilant about people coming to the trackside. But my guess is I already scared him off today, whoever he is. So all I'm saying is keep your eyes open."

"Yeah, OK."

"And if he's from a rival club and if he poaches you, I'll kill him and gouge his eyes out! Followed shortly after by you. After I've dropped you in boiling lead. Got that?"

"Yes, Coach!"

And she went home on the bus, spirits higher. She wasn't bothered by Mr Turner's fears about her being watched by a rival coach. She was flattered. Sport was a kind of performance and performers need an audience.

She wouldn't mention the man to her parents. No point. They'd only worry. And what was there to worry about? And if she did mention it, they couldn't do anything. Except accompany her everywhere. Great.

Definitely best leave it. The rival coach could look all he wanted. Anyway, she had plans, didn't she? And rivalry between clubs didn't feature in them.

Cat got off the bus at her usual stop and began to walk the few hundred yards home. The sun had come out and a strong breeze was washing the clouds away.

Passing the chippy, she had a sudden urge for chips. She went in.

"Chips, please. With salt." Training plans and nutritional regimes were all very well, but normal people like chips.

As she waited, mouth watering at the smell, she looked out of the window. A Blooms van was passing, a woman driving it. Cat cringed at the memory of that huge and horrible spider. She still didn't know who'd sent the flowers. Probably never would.

CHAPTER 21
THE INSECT MAN

THREE weeks have passed since that terrible day in the school science laboratory. It is October now, the light shrinking, sun sinking. The shadows venture further every day, creeping over the city. Professor Bryden has, as expected, lost his job. To be accurate, he has left his job voluntarily. He has simply not returned. Why would he? To be spoken to patronizingly by someone less than half his age, who would no doubt have told him, again, just why his behaviour at the school had been so "inappropriate"? No. No, thank you.

The professor wipes his eyes. The air is cold against his skin, a sudden frost in the air. Leaves are curling and dropping from the trees in the hospital grounds, he notices, though he doesn't care much. He has never liked this time of year. Things coming to an end, insects entering a dead phase. In the old days, he had used this time to go to warmer countries, on research expeditions with his wife. But they were the very old days and now *he* is elderly and he can do nothing like that now. He is not old, not really, but he feels it. Suddenly.

His mind is numbed. That will be the pills working away in his brain, softening it. Changing him. The doctor had been confident, the doctor who'd prescribed them. She'd said the pills would take a while but that they would help.

He does feel numb. He has almost lost his anger. Almost. Still it rises in his throat sometimes, especially when he thinks of that silly girl.

He's seen her once since that day. He was on his bike when he saw her walking along the street with a couple of her school friends and going into her house.

She'll have forgotten him by now. Does she know what has happened to him? Will the silly girl understand or care? What does she know about worry, with her easy family and house with its glossy black door and probably a cleaner to polish the brass letterbox?

At first, he'd thought of trying to teach her a lesson. Somehow. And he'd even had some ideas. Then he'd become ill. Quite suddenly. It had started in the bus queue when he'd seen (though he accepts now that it was not really there) a rare beetle climbing through the blue hair of the woman in front of him. And for the rest of that day he'd kept seeing interesting specimens in unlikely places, until he'd seen an exceptionally beautiful example of a *Mesotopus tarandus* in Waitrose, its shiny black shell quite the glossiest of any stag beetle he'd ever met. But he doesn't want to think about that. It had been very embarrassing. A doctor had been called ... but, no, he will not think about this again. It was a temporary loss of control, caused by panic.

Anyway, now he cares less about teaching the silly girl a lesson. Is that the pills, taking the edge off his anger? In that case, he'd rather not take the pills. He'd rather *feel* his anger in the raw. Because at least anger is real, not this fluffy soft nothingness, this feeling of being wrapped in bedclothes while the world spins by without him.

On the other hand, is he really angry with her now? Could he perhaps forgive her? He almost smiles at that. But smiling is somewhat beyond him now. It's the pills. They take away anger and they take away smiling.

He walks through the hospital grounds, towards the low building where the consulting room waits. He hesitates before walking up the ramp to the door. There is the geranium on the reception windowsill. He'd seen a beautiful caterpillar on it when he'd been there before, but he had not told the doctor woman that, in case she either moved it or told him it wasn't really there. There is the non-smoking sign. There through the frosted glass is the fuzzy shape of the grey-haired receptionist, a woman who annoys him quite considerably. The way she looks at him with a gentle pity and makes cheery conversation for which he has no appetite at all.

He really doesn't want to go in. This numb feeling is all very well. But he does not see the point of it. He still sees insects where logically he knows they could not be. But why should that bother anyone? He likes insects, after all, so it is not a problem. Seeing insects should not be treated as a symptom of illness. It doesn't harm anyone and he enjoys it. He would be fine if people would leave him alone. He could control himself in Waitrose, he knows. He would not make a habit of frightening customers and embarrassing himself.

But he would like to be allowed to *feel*.

There, for example, just sitting on his shoe, its extraordinarily long antennae drifting lazily on a breeze, is a golden leaf-rolling cricket. And there – look! – on his hand as he holds it out and brings it close to his face, is a black and white damselfly, *Megaloprepus coerulatus*. He gazes at it, turning his hand this way and that to see every facet of its impossible beauty.

No, he does not want to lose this. And maybe soon the pills will take this away as well. Not his anger but his reason for being. His insects.

He looks at his watch. Looks at the receptionist's fuzzy head one more time and turns on his heel. Walks quickly away, though not towards his home. He has something to do. He has made a decision.

As he walks off, he stops one more time. Well, he has to. Because in his haste to act on his new decision, he almost steps on an insect. It is walking across the pavement in front of him, towards the road. Now it begins to cross the road, away from him. Brown, speckly, short legs, short antennae, long body. He stops to watch, his mind taking in only its shape and beauty.

An engine. Car. Fast. Too fast.

He darts into the road and scoops the insect out of the way, holding it against his body, shaking his fist at the car as it speeds by bellowing its horn.

He is glad, of course, to have saved this insect. Small as it is, though not defenceless. The most successful animals on earth, as the museum had used to say. His museum.

He puts the insect gently in his pocket before going on his way. First, though, he murmurs its name. He always finds the names of insects to be calming, more calming than any pill that the doctor could have prescribed to him.

"*Xestobium rufovillosum*." The deathwatch beetle. For one of two reasons: because it taps during the silent watch over a dying person or because it is able to predict death. We believe what we wish, he muses to himself.

CHAPTER 22
LOSING CONTROL

JUST after five weeks since the terrible day in the science lab, and Cat's life had settled into normality. And the Danny thing seemed to have faded. Not that she was speaking to him, just that their paths had crossed less. He'd missed fencing this week and had been off school for a few days with some illness. Presumably.

It was towards the end of October, after the holiday week, and the air was sometimes crisp and bright, the ground scrunchy with frost-rimmed leaves, and sometimes dank, sodden, with wet mist clogging the air. Training continued whatever the weather – it just went indoors if necessary. But leaving the house in the damp dark to go swimming was harder than usual and she steeled herself to do it every time, especially during the holiday when half her friends were in sunny places and the rest were sleeping late in the mornings. That Tuesday, she'd pleaded a headache and her mum had let her miss the evening swimming session. She'd stayed cosy in her room and messed around on the internet. Feeling guilty. But mostly cosy.

She still hadn't talked to her parents about cutting back on training. They were often busy or Angus was in the way or the moment just didn't happen. She almost had once, but the opportunity passed and she had let it go.

Wednesday evening, and Cat didn't much feel like going on Phiz. Each time she went on it nowadays, she still imagined that spider, grotesque and huge across the screen, so big you could see the hairs on its legs.

But it was hard *not* to go on Phiz. Everyone else would be on it and she might miss something. Besides, she wouldn't make the same mistake again.

Which did not stop the chill slither down her back when she went on the site and saw that she had a new watcher.

Or the same one back again.

She almost gasped. Everything around her receded and now only the screen remained, and her hands hovering on the keyboard.

It was an insect. A brown beetle. With specks, short legs, short antennae. Nothing special-looking. Oddly, not even particularly horrible. It wasn't what it looked like that was so chilling – it was simply that it was there.

But simple to deal with too and Cat took a deep breath as she moved the mouse onto the Hot or Not spot and clicked very firmly on the word "Not".

The insect disappeared. Immediately and totally.

Cat quickly closed Phiz down. She refused to think about what this meant. She took her folder from her schoolbag and, almost not breathing, forced her eyes to focus on her homework task. Maybe all this would have a good result – more work done. It was not a bad idea. It wasn't a *great* idea, but it had its advantages. She squeezed her mind to concentrate. She would not allow herself to have any thoughts as to who was trying to watch her.

But it was no good. The virus had gone and so had the insect, but if someone was still watching her, he could keep coming back. He couldn't get into her private space if she didn't let him and now she had proper antivirus software he couldn't put a virus on again, but the whole point about Phiz was the open access area, where anyone could see you. How much information had she put there? Had she given away too much? Could she delete some of it, or was it too late?

Feeling cold, she went into her open access profile page. It was all the usual stuff – pet's name, birthday, hobbies, favourite bands, favourite websites, school stuff, sayings, facts from her childhood, things that had happened at school, photos of her at various ages. Favourite things and biggest hates: that's where it said she hated insects. She would take that off, for a start.

But she didn't see how someone could get dangerous information from any of this. If some pervert found her page, he'd discover a lot about her, but not enough to find out where she lived. Except that it was Edinburgh

– well, that wouldn't tell him much. She had never put her address on the site, obviously. There were photos. She took a look at them. When she thought of a stranger viewing them, she felt … watched. Actually, she felt a bit sick. She took some of the photos down. Just in case. There were a couple that might identify her school, she realized. She removed them.

She scrolled through the various pages. Her daily timetable — why had she put that there? But everyone did. It was a Phiz feature. It was supposed to help you feel organized, in control, and let people see how incredibly busy and full your life was. Suddenly, she didn't want everyone to know her training schedules, her after-school activities, the days she went running or cycling or swimming.

Even so, whatever her fears, it was still far more likely that it was Danny, not some pervy stranger.

And he had to have sent the flowers with the spider. She knew she should tell her parents, but then she'd have to tell them so much. And she didn't think she could face that, the reactions, the row, the "how could you be so stupid?" accusations.

Cat couldn't sit still. She stood up, frustrated, fidgety. Oddly, she felt like going for a run. It was horrible outside, cold and wet, and if this had been training she wouldn't have wanted to, but now she really felt the need to run. Fast and hard.

But her parents would want to know why. And they'd be bound to say no in weather like this. And the dark. She put some music on instead. Loud. The Kaiser Chiefs. An angry beat.

Her thoughts jangled. Her coach always said if you tried hard enough you could block out any distraction. But it didn't feel like that. It felt as though things were going on around her, happening to her, that were not in her control.

CHAPTER 23
SACRED DAYS

THURSDAYS after school were sacred. No training, no after-school stuff. Apart from homework, but homework could wait. This was a time for friends. Sometimes, Cat and the others met in a coffee shop, lingering on the sofas for longer than you were supposed to make one drink last. Or they went shopping, coming back in time for tea. Or in the summer they went to the Meadows and lay on the grass and chatted or kicked a ball or took revision notes if school tests were coming up. Not that much work got done.

Cat could not remember a time before this Thursday ritual.

Which explained her reaction when Bethan made her announcement, as they got onto the bus after school that Thursday, on their way to the coffee shop.

"I got a job! A paper round! I'll be rich!"

"But you can't get up in time for school, let alone a

paper round!" said Marcus.

"No, the freebie one. Thursday afternoons."

"But you can't!" said Cat. "Not Thursdays! What about us?"

"Yeah, but I can't say no, can I? I mean, it's money."

"Actually, I have a problem with Thursday too, starting in a couple of weeks," said Ailsa, as they all found seats, squashing up together at the back. "I'm working in a charity shop for my D of E."

Cat wasn't doing the Duke of Edinburgh: she had too much else on, but most of the others had signed up.

She said nothing.

"Let's go to the cinema or something on Saturday afternoon," Ailsa said. "All of us."

"Um, excuse me…" Marcus pushed Ailsa's shoulder.

She looked embarrassed. "Go on, the others can come too, can't they?"

"Sure." He didn't *sound* too sure. And this was obviously supposed to be a date.

"Yeah, we should all go – stop you two getting up to anything," said Bethan.

"What, like talking about computers?" Josh said with a grin.

"I can't come," said Cat, quietly.

"Why?"

"The usual."

"But we're going in the afternoon. After your training ends."

"It's not training. It's a swimming competition. Starts at twelve. And the national selectors will be there."

The others were silent. They looked at each other.

"We can go another time," Bethan said.

"But I want to come with you *now!*" Cat knew she sounded like a small child. But she was sick of this. Constantly considering her training. And now two of her friends were getting jobs and none of them seemed that bothered about meeting up less. But then they were maybe feeling cosy in their pairs. Because that's what they were now, she could see. Bethan and Josh; Ailsa and Marcus. And Cat, the gooseberry. "I'm sick of athletics. I want to get a job too and have money and just hang out with you guys."

"But your mum and dad will be furious!" Bethan looked surprised.

"So? I can't do it for *them*, can I?"

"She's right," said Josh. "Your parents don't get to decide your career."

"But I'd love to be so good at sport," Ailsa said.

"Are you sure? For a hobby, yes, but for your life?"

At their bus stop, they piled off and into the coffee shop. The conversation moved on. The others didn't know what to say and Cat didn't know if she could say anything without getting emotional, which she wasn't going to do. So she kept her mouth shut and tried to join in the chat.

But one thing she decided. She *was* going to tell her parents that night. She would cut back on the training and try to get a part-time job. Even a few hours, just like the others. She *needed* to be just like the others. And her parents couldn't stop her.

And the competition? No one could make her go. Or, if she did, no one could make her swim her best. And if she didn't, she wouldn't be selected. Which would solve the problem. Sort of. It wasn't a great thing to think about but there wasn't an alternative that she could see.

And so, later that evening, at dinner, after helping lay the table and being nice and polite and doing everything right, she began to say what she felt.

CHAPTER 24
TIME TO TALK

IT wasn't as easy as that. You can plan a conversation as much as you like – it doesn't make any difference. Her *planned* conversation went along the lines of: Cat says she's going to try to get a job; brother makes some sarky comment about no one employing her; Cat keeps her cool; parent tells Angus not to be a pain; parents express initial scepticism; parents ask, "What about your training?"; Cat says she wants to take a break from it, just cut back a bit as she's worried that she's overdoing it, maybe needs to cool it for a while till she's older; parents look impressed that she has thought so maturely about it; one parent – probably her father – says it seems reasonable, that it would be bad for her to overdo it; mother disagrees but father talks her round; they agree to compromise in some way – or, more likely, talk about it later.

Meanwhile, Cat is *not* specifically told she can't look

for a job so she silently takes it that she *can*. She smiles secretly and looks forward to Saturday, when she will note down all the vacancy signs on her way to athletics and then deliberately not impress the selectors at the competition.

What actually happened was this.

Cat carefully and politely raised the possibility that she might look for a part-time job because all her friends were.

"Who'd give *you* a job?" asked Angus, taking two more potatoes.

"What about your training?" asked her mum.

"And schoolwork," added her dad.

"You're too young." Mum.

"Wait till you're sixteen." Dad.

"So that's a 'no' then? Just like that?" said Cat, angry already.

"Well, come on, Catty – how can you possibly fit a job in with everything you do?"

"But I want to *stop* doing some of it. That's the point. I want to cut down the training." It was out. She held her breath.

"You can't be serious!" Her dad.

"You've got a great career in front of you. You can't turn your back on your talent." Mum.

"What will your coach say? He believes in you." Dad.

"I don't CARE what he thinks! It's not his life, or yours. It's mine! And I'm sick of all the training and the pressure. I don't want to do it any more."

"Don't be silly. This is too sudden – you don't have to decide now. You can't throw it all away on a whim."

Her mum wore an irritating fake-sympathetic smile. Her dad took another mouthful of wine. Angus was eating with his mouth open and grinning. Cat scowled at him and looked away. Actually, she wanted to hit him.

"It's not a whim. I've been thinking it for ages. All my friends…"

"Oh, '*all my friends*' – that old one!"

Her dad spoke. "It's your life, not your friends'. Your friends will soon enough find their own paths but you've a talent you can't ignore."

"I didn't ask for it! I don't want it! Just because Grandpa did it; why do I have to?"

"It's nothing to do with Grandpa. That's not why… Is that what you really think?"

"Yes, actually. You're always going on about it – him." Her mum looked hurt, her dad bewildered. "But I just want to be the same as everyone else. I only want to get a few hours' work – anyone would think I was dropping out of school or something. I could be taking drugs. Or shoplifting. Or getting pissed every night."

Furious silence. Then Angus's phone rang in his pocket.

"Get that phone out of here!" their dad shouted. And Angus slouched away, answering the phone while slowly and deliberately taking his plate to the kitchen.

Her mum looked at her. "Listen, Catty, let's talk

about this later, shall we? You can't rush a big decision like that. I think you're maybe just feeling a bit jaded. Just a phase."

"And if you feel the same way later then we'll see," said her dad.

Oh, 'we'll see'? That old one.

"How much later?"

"Maybe after Christmas."

Cat scraped her chair back and stood up. She couldn't look at them. "Oh, just forget it! I *knew* you wouldn't understand. And I'll still feel the same after Christmas, I guarantee you. Except that before then I'll have lost my friends. And I'll have huge muscles like some frumpy weightlifter."

"Don't be so melodramatic, Catriona. Of course you won't lose your friends. You might get different ones. Things change."

"I don't want different ones! How can you say that?" She stamped out of the room, flinging the door shut behind her, wincing at the crash of it, and ran upstairs. Noticing that her mum had not denied the weightlifter bit.

CHAPTER 25
NO RESOLUTION

IN her bedroom, Cat fumed. She couldn't go on Phiz – she knew her mum would be up at any moment to continue the discussion. Her mum would never let things go.

She picked up her trainers and threw them at the fireplace, where they landed with a clatter among the candles. Catching sight of herself in the mirror she stared briefly. Horrible. Scowling, twisted mouth. And her hair all limp and rat's-taily – enough to put her in a bad mood on its own.

Cat bent down and let her hair hang towards the floor in front of her as she brushed air into it. When she stood up straight again, it fell thick and blonde round her face. It wasn't bad hair. Given a chance it could be one of her assets. And it *was* at the beginning of each day when she went to school, or if she was going out somewhere or had had a chance to deal with it. But when she did athletics… With both hands now she pulled it back off her face, scraping it into the tight ponytail she had to wear for running. Now her ears stuck out and her nose looked more pointed. Not a great look. She shook her hair free again and brushed it back to thickness.

Everywhere in her room were reminders of athletics. Trophies. Trainers. Running spikes. Boring untrendy tracksuits. A swimming costume twisted on the radiator. Certificates. A swimming hat, towel. Her kitbag. Two water bottles lying on the floor. Both unwashed. The calendar with the club logo – and all the competitions highlighted in purple. Even the ruler she'd been using for fencing practice.

Was she imagining it or was there a faint breath of chlorine in the air?

Did she actually smell of swimming pools and sweat?

And those muscles – they looked bigger than last week. A runner had nice lean long muscles but all the swimming she was doing was giving her a top-heavy bulk. She'd not really noticed it much before but now, every time she looked in the mirror, her eyes seemed to be drawn to her arms and shoulders.

Her mum knocked and came in when Cat mumbled an answer.

"Can we talk?"

"Is there any point?"

"I think so."

"Go on then. You're the psychiatrist."

"Clever-clever."

"Come on, Mum: what are you going to say apart from repeat what you've already said?"

"I don't want us to argue about it. I just think it's a very hasty decision and I think you might regret it. It's easy to feel frustrated or bored or fed up if you sometimes have to train when you don't want to, but you know it's the only way to succeed."

"But I don't know if I want it any more."

"It's only natural to have doubts."

"It's more than that. I have to really want it and I don't know if I do."

"And another thing – it's not about Grandpa, you know. He *would* be proud of you, of course he would. But you have to do it for yourself."

"Exactly! That's the whole point."

"Do you remember the feeling of winning the other week? And all the other times? You know you love it."

"I know but … it's all the training."

"It'll be worth it. You'll see."

"It might not! I might easily not succeed. I might not get picked on Saturday or I might get picked and a year down the line get an injury or just not win or whatever. What then?"

"You'll have your other subjects too. You're good at history and English and there are lots of other subjects you could do at university. No one's saying you should only do athletics. But you have a gift and you should use it. I bet you'll regret it if you give up now."

"But…"

"I think you maybe just need a bit of a push."

"No: I get pushed all the time! That's the problem. I want to be normal. I want to get a job, Mum, like the others. Just for a few hours a week."

"Why don't you be my personal trainer? I'd pay you! Look at this flab, Catty. I need your help!" And her mum grabbed a wodge of flesh at her waist.

Cat looked away. She wished her mum wouldn't do that – it was normally only after Christmas or a holiday that Cat got the wodge-grabbing and wailing about being too fat.

"That's not the same. That's just pretend – not a proper job. I want to work in a shop or something. Why can't I?"

"You're probably not old enough. Don't you have to be sixteen or something?"

"But other people do, just a few hours – there's ways you can do that. Even a paper round. Washing up in a café. Anything. Why do you and Dad have to be so boring and uptight about stuff? I thought you'd be glad I wanted to get a job. Responsibility and all that."

"Look, we'll think about it, OK? If you find something, and if it doesn't interfere with everything else, then we'll think about it. Honestly. Now can I please borrow your bike tomorrow? And your helmet."

"Friday's hockey. *Remember?*" She glared at her mum.

"No, you haven't. *Remember?*"

Cat remembered – no hockey because it was some

year group's parents' evening. She grunted.

Her mum rolled her eyes. "So can I borrow your bike? Please?"

"I suppose."

"Well, you don't want me to be a fat slob of a mother, do you? Or drop dead of a heart attack in my prime."

Cat couldn't be bothered to do her usual style of reply. *Bit late for that*, would have been one.

"Don't be cross, Catty. It'll work out, you'll see. You won't lose your friends and the world won't end. But dreams are worth following."

She touched Cat's head as she left the room. Cat mumbled a reply.

Tears pricked her eyes. But she wiped them away angrily and vowed to follow her plan. She *would* find a job and she would slowly drop back on the athletics. Maybe cut the swimming and biathlon stuff and just run.

As she heard her mum's footsteps reach the ground floor, a sudden thought hit her. The brakes on her bike were dodgy. She'd been meaning to tell her parents but hadn't got round to it.

"Mum!" she called. No reply. Her mum must have gone into the kitchen already.

Never mind – she'd tell her at breakfast.

CHAPTER 26
A PSYCHIATRIST'S LIFE

DIANA McPherson pushed a strand of blonde hair back into place. It had been a difficult day, as so often on a Friday. Her patient, David Sorley, was supposed to be going home. Only he didn't have a home to go to. His parents couldn't take him. Couldn't? Wouldn't. She didn't really blame them. After all, they had two other kids to think about and David was twenty-two. Twenty-two years old, unemployed, and suffering his first episode of schizophrenia. He wasn't the worst case she'd come across, nowhere near that. But any case was bad enough for the people who loved him.

Poor David. And his family. Nice family too, by all accounts. She'd met the parents, shock still draining their faces, shock that this was where they were — a grim psych unit in a grim hospital that tried to pretend that it wasn't grim by placing a few strategic geraniums. They'd been unable to understand how this could have happened to their son. Had his earlier cannabis use played a part? She'd agreed that it possibly had. Though they should not blame themselves, she'd said. Or should they? Maybe they should. Maybe they hadn't been tough enough. Or too tough. One or the other, who knew?

But today, her task had been to tell them that he couldn't stay in the hospital. They were worried about what he would do if he came home. Schizophrenia was frightening, and they'd read plenty of newspaper stories. He could be dangerous, they said.

She couldn't be *sure* he wasn't dangerous. But he was taking his medication and he seemed to be doing well. There was nothing more she could do while he was responding to treatment, not unless he became violent, which he hadn't. He'd been out a few times with supervision and, apart from one minor incident when he'd panicked a bit, he'd been no problem. Nothing since then.

So she'd ended up spending too much time that day persuading him that he would be fine out of the hospital – as long as he took his medication and came back for follow-up appointments – and sorting out his care plan. The team had worked hard to find accommodation for him. They had found a hostel but it wasn't adequate. She knew that and he probably knew that too. But she'd had to pretend she thought it was.

David had wanted to stay in the hospital, cared for. He felt safer. He was frightened about the voices coming back.

"But the pills keep the voices away. You know that,

David," Diana had said.

"But they might not," he'd said, pushing the straggly hair from his eyes and tucking it into that knitted hat he always wore. His face was thin. He should eat more. He needed someone to care for him. But who would do that? She'd sensed that the mother would have, but the father had put his foot down. Understandably.

He was lost. She knew that and it hurt. It wasn't what she'd intended when she trained. She'd planned to cure people, find clever paths through their extraordinary and fascinating minds. Funny how things didn't turn out as you'd hoped.

Then someone had discovered that David had an uncle near by. Presumably he hadn't said so before because he knew that would be a reason not to stay in hospital. But they'd contacted this uncle, who'd said it was no problem – apparently he'd spent a lot of time with David recently. Members of the team made sure this uncle understood everything and could deal with the medication. And would see that David came back for follow-ups.

Now more than an hour after she had eventually said goodbye to David, and seen his lost eyes for one last time, she packed her things into her bag ready to go home. She'd checked with the staff that he'd be signed out properly and collected by the uncle. And she put David from her mind until his next appointment.

Outside, wind scurried the leaves along the pavement. She remembered a comedy programme she'd seen once, with a sketch involving a pile of leaves that followed a woman home along the pavement. Although it had been very funny, it had also been frightening: the eerie leaves with a mind of their own, chasing the woman in Hitchcock fashion along the empty street. She couldn't remember what had happened in the end – perhaps the leaves overpowered the woman and smothered her to death or something. It didn't really matter.

She was the last to leave the unit, setting the lock on the door before pulling it shut behind her. The street was empty, twilight settling on the leaf-strewn pavements and hanging in the thinning trees. This was partly hospital grounds, partly public road. Cars were usually few, though fast, ignoring the ten miles per hour signs.

The smell of hops from the brewery was rich this evening and she breathed deeply. It was an Edinburgh smell that she loved.

Diana squeezed her bag inside the rucksack she'd borrowed from Cat that morning, as she'd set off on her short cycle to work. The cycling – suggested by her daughter some weeks ago because Diana was moaning about being unfit – rarely actually happened. There was always a reason not to: the weather, a meeting, tiredness. But today she had vowed to do it, appalled by the extra layer of flesh she'd been aware of all week. "Muffin top," as Angus had helpfully said.

Diana had already changed into her jeans for the purpose of her return journey. The actual route home was too short to be worthwhile, but she was going to head in another direction and cycle for about half an hour before coming home.

Her daughter had explained the circuit to her when she'd first suggested cycling. It was based on the route Cat usually did on a Friday evening. Cat always took her bike to school on Fridays, so that after hockey she could do this testing ride involving the university campus on the hill. Exposed for most of the way, it was quite safe and Diana and Bill had been reasonably happy for her to do it, though she should stop now for the winter: the clocks would go back this weekend, Diana realized, and it would be much darker next week.

Of course, Cat had planned an easier version of the route for her mother, who had only cycled a couple of times since starting the new fitness kick.

"Don't want you to kill yourself," Bill had teased.

"You could do with coming yourself," Diana had retorted. And it was true. He wasn't exactly the hard-muscled, athletic being she'd married. They could both do with getting fitter. It was just that the time never seemed right.

Today, the time had seemed right. Or unavoidable. Cat didn't need her bike because she didn't have hockey, though she'd given her permission rather grudgingly the night before, Diana thought. Teenage strop, and a bit of frustration about too much training. She'd get over it. Diana didn't want to pressurize Cat too much but everyone needed a push now and then. It was a parent's duty, wasn't it? Besides, wouldn't anyone need a push to get out of bed for the early morning swims that Cat did several times a week?

And Cat's grandfather, Diana's father, *would* have been proud. "Don't just follow your dreams," he'd have said. "Grab them with both hands and pull yourself towards them." She remembered the glitter in his eyes when she was a little girl and he'd talked to her about running, and the sheer joy of winning. Not that she'd been that interested then. She'd never been one for running herself. Sweat was unattractive and unpleasant.

There was a lot of him in Catriona, she thought. Determination, fire. Which was why she'd been so surprised at that outburst of doubt yesterday. It was so unlike her. Maybe they shouldn't push her so hard. But how were you to know what was right? Too much or too little: you couldn't know until it was too late.

Diana had left the house earlier than usual that morning, before the kids were up, and had wobbled the short distance to work. In the few times she'd done the journey so far, she had discovered something painful about cobbles and bikes. She'd not yet relearned her ancient cycling skills.

But she'd got there. Safely. And now, work finished, she was going to do what she had planned to do: Cat's evening route. Or Cat, Bill and Angus would never let her forget it.

She placed Cat's neon yellow helmet on her head. Flicked the bike lights on. And set off. Left onto the main road. Along to the big junction. Left again. She hadn't known this was a hill. It had looked quite flat from the driving seat of a car. Wind in her face. Against her. Sweating already. Breath painful in her throat. Cars roaring up behind. A heavy feeling in her legs. But she would do it. She changed gears and it became easier. She could do this.

The brakes seemed sticky but she could cope. Maybe just use her foot if necessary.

At the university campus, she followed Cat's instructions and didn't go far up the hill, took the easy route. And then down again. Bit scary with the sticky brakes, but she wasn't going too fast: she knew she could stop easily enough. Wind in her face again. Always against her. How? But this time downhill. Exhilaration. A long, lonely road sweeping round. Onto Morningside Road, past the traffic lights, another hill, a bad one this time, possibly the need to stop. But no, she *could* do it.

She did it.

Turning left. Flat road now. Her legs like lead even so. This was horrible. She really didn't like this. Why did people like to get sweaty? Well, at least she could have a glass of wine without feeling guilty.

And now there she was near the psych hospital, almost back where she'd started. If she turned left she'd be at work, but this was Friday, the weekend, time to relax. So, glad to be nearly home, Diana turned right, as Cat would have done at pretty much the same time every Friday, being quicker than her mother and having done a longer route.

Diana probably did see the thin figure peer out from the lane on her right as she approached quite slowly. But she wouldn't have thought anything of it. Just someone smoking or something. She didn't have time to take in whether she recognized the face. The thin face, the long straggly hair. And by the time the figure had leapt out, it was too late to stop, or even begin to apply the brakes, or turn, or avoid her assailant. Or even scream.

Her world went black.

CHAPTER 27
HOSPITAL SMELLS

THE phone call when it came was horrible. Her father's anguished, "Oh my God!" as he listened to the voice on the other end. Followed by the words, "Yes … yes … where? Are you sure?" Cat had been on the landing and had heard. She hurled herself down the stairs. Angus ran out of his bedroom. And then their father spoke the shocking words, "Mum's had an accident. I have to go to the hospital." A blinding panic flooded through her.

"We're coming!" said Angus.

"No, you've got to stay here."

"You can't leave us, Dad!"

"What's happened to her?" asked Cat.

"She fell off her bike. Hit her head."

Cat grabbed the banister. "We have to come, please, Dad!" She wanted to ask how serious it was, but she just couldn't.

Angus asked. Their father shook his head harshly,

pulling on his coat, fumbling for his wallet, phone, keys. Grabbed the dog lead, stared at it, put it in his pocket. Took it out again and dropped it on the stairs. "They don't know or can't say, I don't know. She's in A&E and she's having tests. Come on – get your coats. Cat, check the back door. Quick!"

So she wasn't dead. She wasn't dead. She wasn't dead. Having tests. What tests? Like X-rays? Not in Intensive Care then. But what did Cat know? She was clutching at straws but somehow she couldn't take in the fear.

And the horrible, black, heart-clutching realization that she had not told her mum about the brakes.

One minute of rushing round the house, locking up, getting phones, leaving lights on, and they were on their way. Little was said in the car. Their dad's curse when the traffic lights were against them was almost silent, bottled up inside. Fifteen minutes with each of them hidden away in lonely thoughts. Every now and then, their dad would say things like, "It'll be OK; they'd have said if she wasn't. Wouldn't they?" It was as though all his own professionalism went out of the window and he knew no more than them. They needed him to know more, to be reassuring.

"She'll be OK, won't she, Dad?" asked Angus, his voice small and tight.

"Course she will. Amazing what they can do nowadays."

Angus turned and looked out of the window. Was he reassured? Cat knew that she wasn't. Her brain felt frozen.

The hospital: new, white, smart. Full of the latest technology, it must be. Huge car park, no space near the A&E entrance. Sudden fury from their dad as he realized how far from the doors he'd have to park. Parked. Sorted ticket. All of them running towards the entrance. Three smokers outside, one in a hospital gown. Looking at them with some kind of pity. Through the doors, which slid slowly open in a delayed reaction. And now his authority as a doctor took over as he explained quickly who they were and asked to be taken to Diana McPherson straight away.

They were asked to sit in the waiting area, where a shambling drunk with dirty grey jogging bottoms shouted abuse at a fat boy and his mother, who were kicking the vending machine because it wouldn't give up the cola they claimed to have paid for. Three people had blood on them, one with a closed and bloodied eye. Most were silent. One small child sniffed repeatedly, exhausted in his mother's arms.

Cat and Angus sat, outwardly numb, as they waited. Their father would not wait. He was about to storm over to the desk to argue, when a young man in a white coat called them over. Cat studied his face. Was that a smile? If it was, was it a smile of welcome, of reassurance, or of pity?

Their father asked, immediately, "How is she?"

"She's going to be fine. Broken wrist, few bumps and bruises: nothing we can't fix."

A wave, a storm of relief.

"You're sure?"

"She's going to be fine."

Cat felt involuntary tears behind hot eyes. She turned to Angus with a crinkled smile. Their dad took them each by the hand – something he had not done for a long time – and they all followed the young doctor towards a cubicle at the end, its curtain open. And then Cat wanted to cry more, when she saw her mother lying there, hair in a mess, arm in a sling, fingers swollen, blood roughly wiped from her face and a couple of white strips across a cut on her cheek. Her eyes were closed, but opened as soon as they came in.

"Sorry, guys," she said, her voice trembling.

"What have you been up to, Di? I knew we shouldn't have let you out on your own!"

Cat could see the helmet on top of a white plastic bag under the bed. It had a huge dent in it which she preferred not to think about.

"Sorry about your bike, Catty."

"Mum, I'm so sorry, I..."

"It wasn't your fault. Just because it was your bike." Her mum winced and cradled her arm.

"But, Mum, the brakes, they were sticking. I forgot..."

"The brakes were fine – I'd noticed they were sticky but I wasn't going fast and I could easily put my foot down. Don't..."

"Don't talk, Diana," said the doctor.

"I'm still sorry, Mum." They smiled at each other.

Angus was subdued, looking round at the machines. Some wires disappeared under her gown, and a thin tube went into her arm. It wasn't easy seeing her lie there, not walking around giving orders and organizing things. One of those grey cardboard basins sat by the bed, in case she was sick.

The doctor spoke now, as a nurse came to check the various gadgets and write something on a chart. "Never mind about the bike – I'm sure it can be fixed. Just like your mum's wrist. The X-ray shows a simple fracture, but we'll get that patched up." He turned to their father. "She's going to be fine, Dr McPherson; bit of concussion, so she'll need a few days of rest, but you'll know about all that. She should be signed off work for at least a week. Psychiatrist: well, she'll know enough about heads then, won't you, Diana?"

Cat's mum smiled slightly, out of politeness. Cat wanted to touch her hair, wanted to hold her hand, wanted to have a hug. But she couldn't do any of those things. The doctor continued, "We'd like to keep her in tonight, but we're not expecting any problems. The X-ray is clear – no skull fracture. We're doing fifteen minute observations, just routine."

"What happened, Di? Seriously?"

She moistened her lips with her tongue. "I don't remember. I was nearly home, and I was just about to pass the lane, and I was feeling pretty tired, but then, nothing. No idea. But not the brakes, honestly, Catty." She winced again as pain crossed her face.

"Quiet now," said the nurse. "We're going to get your wrist sorted very soon. Just lie back. Wiggle your toes. Think of somewhere nice, lying on a beach or somewhere."

Cat knew her mother would not find the idea of lying on a beach particularly relaxing. She wasn't a beach-lying sort of person. Too sandy. Cat wanted to tell the nurse.

And what the hell was the point of wiggling your toes?

Their father turned to the doctor. "Was a car involved? Did anyone see anything?"

"Not as far as we know. A passer-by found her, probably only a few moments later. She was conscious but it sounds as though she had lost consciousness, probably very briefly. There were no witnesses, as far as we know."

"Just need more practice, Mum," said Angus.

"A few weeks for that wrist to heal, and you'll be back in the saddle, no problem."

Diana shook her head, then groaned and closed her eyes. Her family said quick goodbyes and were ushered out of the cubicle. Cat took a last look at her mother lying there, so vulnerable, pale, older.

Their father would come back again later, he said, and then tomorrow to collect her. Meanwhile, he would take Cat and Angus home.

In the car, Cat had to ask, "She will definitely be OK, won't she? I mean she was unconscious: she might get bleeding in the brain or something, mightn't she?"

"She'll be fine, I promise. They'll keep an eye out for any symptoms but they're obviously not expecting anything."

"Will she remember more about what happened?"

"She might. In time. But it doesn't sound as though there was much to remember. It'll just be one of those things. The road's bad there; she'll have gone over a bump or something. Anyway, the main thing is she's going to be OK. Get one of my CDs, will you, Angus? I need Pink Floyd."

He turned the volume up and soon the fast beat filled the car. They all retreated into their own thoughts. Shock had turned to relief and Cat felt exhausted.

She found it hard to sleep that night. Later, long after her dad had come back for the second time and had come in to say good night to her, reassuring her further that her mum would be fine, she got up from her bed and walked to the window.

She looked out into the blustery thick night. She needed air. Opening the window wide, she leaned her elbows on the sill and let the wind blow hard through her hair and into the room. A few papers flew off the table behind her, but she didn't mind. She had a good view from here, and with so many leaves fallen she could see lights blinking in windows far and near. But she looked down at the street now, at its mustard light, its dark corners by the bins, at the familiar cars parked in their familiar places. A cat – or maybe a fox, yes, definitely a fox – slipped along the top of the wall.

A cyclist spun past, seeming to slow a little as he came level with their house. And then the man was gone. For it was a man, she was sure, in a bulky coat, collar up, no helmet.

He should wear a helmet, she thought. Think what would have happened to her mum if she had not. That horrible crushed dent in the plastic. It didn't bear thinking about.

Cat shivered, closed the window, and went back to bed.

CHAPTER 28
SWIMMING

"**WHAT** are you doing, Catriona?" Her dad shuffled into the kitchen in slippers, his greying hair tousled and his eyes dark and drawn.

"What?"

"Why are you in sports kit?"

"It's Saturday." Cat was in the kitchen the morning after the accident, eating breakfast and chucking oats for Polly to catch.

"You don't have to go, you know. Not today. You must be tired after last night."

Typical. You say you don't want to do something and they say you've got to. You say you're going to do it and they say you don't need to. But she wanted to. She had to. She felt guilty. It was stupid, she knew that – her mum had said the accident was nothing to do with the brakes. But Cat knew that she should have remembered to tell her. She should have cared more. What if...?

"It's a swimming competition, Dad."

"God, I'd forgotten. But I can't take you. I have to go to the hospital. I'm so sorry…"

"It's OK – I can get the bus."

"Are you sure? I feel really bad I can't come and watch, but…" and the word hung in the air, his face tired, creased.

"I'm sure."

Later, on the bus, she got a text from Bethan. *"Can we come 2 watch?"* Her heart leapt. So they weren't going to the cinema or whatever: they were coming to see her.

"yes if not 2 boring!"

"c u l8r good luck!"

Cat could not risk losing friends like Bethan and Ailsa: friends who understood her and knew what she'd be thinking. Friends were more important than dreams of future glory.

She got off the bus and jogged the last short distance to the Commonwealth pool. She could see the other teams arriving, piling off the buses, their coaches clucking around them. She recognized club colours from previous competitions, and some individual faces. Rivals.

A familiar stomach-churn of nervousness. The adrenalin was beginning, making her legs spring, her whole body feel light. She had to do well. She could pretend she was doing this for her mother or for guilt, but in fact she was doing it for herself.

She was trapped by the need to do it. The need not to fail.

She *would* cut back on the effort … but later. She couldn't deliberately lose a race. If she was selected for anything further, like the national squad, she could always say no. Postpone till the next year. Something would turn up. But lose deliberately? Simply not an option. She didn't know how she could ever have thought she might.

Cat joined her team and even seeing them was part of it. She might not like them but it was her team – and she was the star of it. Her swimming coach, a small sturdy man called Jim, was talking to the judges. Mr Turner came over to Cat, grinning and looking important.

"Ready to win today, Catriona? Ready to put everything into it? Sleep well? Eat well?" Mr T. might not be her swimming coach but she was his club star and he was in charge of her biathlon training. And he was senior to Jim.

She didn't tell Mr T. or anyone that last night her mum could have died. The head injury could have been so much worse. When she thought of it she felt cold, sick, so she didn't want to think about it. Let alone have to tell the story.

After changing into her costume, Cat didn't see her friends while she was warming up and receiving all the last-minute instructions from both Jim and Mr Turner. The spectators' area was slowly filling up, with parents and supporters, the odd journalist, all the hangers-on. Normally her own parents would be there. It was fine that they weren't. They would have to get used to not watching her in competitions.

Officials were everywhere, as always. She called them robots. They never smiled, but spent their lives watching whether a swimmer's fingers touched the right bit of the pool; how many strokes were swum before surfacing after a turn; whose toes were not quite in line at the start: tiny details that were the whole meaning of their little lives.

Cat won her first heats easily. Butterfly and freestyle at her usual lengths. She won the 100m and 200m individual medleys. And her butterfly final. By a mile. She heard Bethan's voice shrieking above the others in the clapping that followed that race. Glowing, she went back to the bench, floating, and was wrapped up in the towel that Mr T. held out to her with a satisfied smile and a few words of praise. It was easy to feel nothing else mattered. But it did. Her mum was alive. The faulty brakes had not caused the accident. She was part of the way to paying for her forgetfulness. If she could win her 400m freestyle too…

As soon as she had a chance, she scanned the spectators to find her friends. Waved at them. They waved wildly back. Ailsa, Bethan, Josh and Marcus – all of them were there. Emily and Rebecca too. They held up a banner. *GO CAT GO!!!* She grinned and they did a thumbs-up sign back.

There was a long time to wait till her freestyle final. She kept warm, occasionally doing stretches, watching the other races, cheering when appropriate, listening to

Jim and Mr T. with half an ear, eating and drinking what she was told, feeling looked after. Focused.

Cat was about to turn back to watch a race and cheer her team, when her eye caught a familiar figure in the crowd. Or not so much the figure but the coat. It was the man again. Looking at her? Maybe not. Could be looking at anyone. He could even be one of the talent spotters.

It was time for her final. She knew what she had to do. And the knot in her stomach as she went towards the pool edge was very familiar. There was a slight nausea. A tingling in her fingers, cold sweat under her arms. The feeling that everyone was watching her. She shivered, shaking her arms and wrists to keep them loose.

Lights glinted, reflecting on windows and water. Flashbulbs. "Go, Cat, Go!" she heard. Cat shielded her eyes as she looked towards the spectators again. She couldn't see the man, but there were a lot of people there. He would be somewhere, watching. She had to do well. No, she had to win. She took a deep breath, and clenched her teeth and silently thought the words, *Do it, do it, do it. Only the best is enough.*

She balanced, poised on the edge, toes gripping, ready to crouch and push as far as she could. The whistle blew and she dived, slicing perfectly into the water. She forced everything from her mind except her strategy, drummed into her over the weeks of training.

Distantly through the surging water and her own breathing, she heard the shouting from the spectators, thought she heard Bethan and the others but put them from her mind. She focused on her body, drawing on all her strength, imagined each muscle working perfectly. Visualized winning, control, strength, as though by thinking it she could conjure victory.

Here came the edge of the pool, time to turn; she tucked her chin in, flipped her body and kicked off strongly from the wall. Speared through the water, surfacing, never losing her rhythm. And rhythm was important – damaging it would lose her valuable fractions of a second. Another turn. And another. She knew she was swimming well, with no loss of power. Energy surged through her. After another flip and twist, she was more than halfway through the race. Three lengths to go.

Soon it would be time to increase speed. But not too soon, not too soon.

Another turn, less perfect than the first. She could see she was up with the front swimmers, possibly in the lead but she couldn't be sure. Increase the speed ... now!

The spectators were a blur, spattered with flecks of colour, sudden reds, flashes of light, waves of movement. She must ignore them, keep them blurred. They had nothing to do with her. She powered on, twisting her body through the water.

But as she turned one last time, she saw him. The man, standing near the judges, away from the other spectators. Watching intently. Notebook in hand. Watching *her*? She knew he was. Simply knew it.

Her heart raced. Every gram of strength now,

everything went into her surge for the far end of the pool. She knew there were other swimmers alongside her – at least two level or almost level with her. She could see the churning water, see the spattered goggles of the one on her left each time she turned her face to breathe, see the muscles of shoulders, the gaping mouth. Focused on every bit of herself: fingers tight together, toes working, each muscle squeezing the tiniest extra bit of speed and strength. She felt good, strong. Her body might be tired but her strength of will would keep it going until the very last moment. Her heart sang as she surged towards the end.

Stretch the fingers – both hands – touch! She grabbed the side of the pool, supported herself gasping, exhausted, looking round. Three other swimmers had finished at almost the same time. She shook hands with the ones on each side. She must have won! She felt it. Looked towards her coach. He was looking at the board. Had she won?

Cat knew from the movement of his body. Then she too saw the screen. Every pleasure drained from her. She couldn't believe it. Rewind. It was a mistake. She *must* have won! By a whisker, but still. Surely?

She hadn't. She'd come third. As she hauled her tired body from the pool, it was an effort to smile. Several of her competitors congratulated her. But she hadn't won. Winning a bronze medal was not winning. Mr T. was coming towards her with her towel.

"Good effort, girl," said Mr T. But his voice had no

passion in it, no gleam. "It was a good speed – a fraction off your personal best. You swam a good race, Catriona. Really."

Really. She couldn't speak. Her legs now felt horribly weak and heavy.

"Hey, don't be like that!" he said. If he didn't shut up she was going to cry. She tried to smile but it didn't come. Her mouth didn't seem to want to do the smiley thing. "You lost by a fraction, a tiny fraction. You can improve by that much, easily – one of your turns could have been tighter. We can work on that. Don't worry, you're on course. And you're younger than them, by nearly two years. They're both out of the Under-16s soon."

And there was Jim, saying much the same. "We can improve that, Catriona, fret not," he said with a smile. "There are good races and there are great races. You swam some great races today. But sometimes it's someone else's day." And he went to talk to someone else.

Cat looked up at the spectators as she went back to the swimmers' area. Her friends weren't looking. They were chatting among themselves. The banner was draped over their knees.

Only the relays were left. Cat's team won theirs and Cat knew she'd swum well. But it didn't feel good enough. The swimmers who'd beaten her before weren't in the relay. The times weren't particularly brilliant, nothing for the selectors to get excited about. One of

Cat's team made a mistake on one of the takeovers, and they had only won because the other teams had either made worse mistakes or simply not been as fast.

Three individual gold medals and a bronze, as well as the relay gold medal. Hardly something to feel down about. Most people would be thrilled. But Cat had put every effort into the race she'd lost, and if she put every effort in and couldn't win, then what could she do? How many times would she have to deal with the kick-in-the-stomach feeling of not winning? Often, was the answer – every athlete did, and the higher she flew, the further it would be to fall.

She wanted to go home. Making an excuse about needing to fetch something from the changing room, Cat went and hid there for a few moments, listening to the echoing shouts from the swimming area. She breathed in the smell of chlorine, the steam, the familiar feeling of heat and yet chill at the same time. The wet floor was clammy underfoot, slippery with other people's skin and soap and sweat. In the mirror, she saw her face, thin wet hair flattened from the hat she'd been wearing, and beneath it the broad shoulders.

She loved it and hated it: this place, this smell, the winning and losing, the always knowing you could do better next time, the dreams. She felt part of it and yet alone. Because you were. You might be part of a team but actually you were doing it for yourself. And if you weren't you'd never do it. You'd never put the effort in.

She went back to the poolside.

Mr T. wasn't there. She looked round. He should be there: the medals were going to be presented. Jim was gathering his swimmers together. There was the announcement. She and the other winners from her team made their way over to the judges' desk. There were the girls who'd beaten her.

The ceremony passed in a blur. She could see Bethan and the others, waving now, and cheering too. And of course she felt proud when she received her medals. But she'd tasted better — a few weeks before, when she'd broken records at the biathlon. Should she be satisfied with third best? And the hope of one day being the best, but maybe never getting there?

Where was Mr Turner? As she stepped off the podium for the last time, she saw him, hurrying towards her. He grabbed her arm, the sinews on his neck standing out in his excitement.

"They're interested in you, Catriona McPherson! They want you to go to a national training camp, in the holidays, with all the best facilities. There's no promises but this is a fantastic chance, Catriona! Well done, you brilliant kid!" And there was Jim in the background, grinning at her before being grabbed by someone else's parent.

Cat could see others looking in her direction. A girl who'd beaten her, turning away now, going off to her own coach. But Cat was being herded by Mr Turner over to the changing area. He was still talking, about training programmes and how much care the squad would take of her. And, yes, her heart was singing; yes, it was a fantastic feeling, being wanted.

That was when she saw the man. "Mr T., look – there's that man again. The one who was watching? I saw him earlier too."

Her coach looked where she was pointing.

"Don't worry about him. I've discovered who he is. I was right – he's from another club. Spying. But he's too late. The selectors want you to stay in this club – we've got it all mapped out. You're stuck with me, kid. You're mine! I'm going to make you a star. All our plans are coming together. It's fantastic, girl!"

But the fear. Fear of losing. Fear of the future. Fear of being trapped.

There was nothing better than winning. And nothing worse than losing. And how did you solve that?

CHAPTER 29
DANNY BEHAVING ODDLY

CAT'S mum came home from the hospital on Saturday evening, fragile and pale. She went straight to her bed. She slept most of Sunday too. But on Sunday evening, she had begun to remember more of her accident. There'd been a person, she thought, someone who had lunged towards her and made her fall. Cat's dad had insisted that the police come to take a statement, which they did, reluctantly. He was furious that they seemed to care so little, but the two police officers who called round explained that with no description, and no witnesses, and the victim suffering from concussion, there was no chance of solving the crime. If there was a crime, they'd said pointedly. It was only her mum's white-faced insistence on dropping it that stopped her dad from becoming quite rude.

"Maybe I was wrong," she said later. "False memory or something. It's easily done."

By Monday, everyone at school had heard about the accident. The story became exaggerated as it went from person to person, especially after Cat had told a couple of people that her mum thought someone might have leapt out at her. So the story grew into rumours of attempted murder. Near the psychiatric hospital; probably one of the patients. Well, it was more interesting to everyone than "fell off her bike".

On Tuesday, Danny didn't come into school again. Apparently, he was ill. Though someone said family problems.

Did he have family problems? Not as far as Cat knew. She'd met his mum, dad and older sister and thought his family seemed really nice – straightforward. More than could be said for him with his insects. Maybe he *was* ill.

She wouldn't say she was exactly bothered.

On Wednesday Cat saw him at registration. He didn't look at her, seemed to move aside when she found herself accidentally walking towards him. She wasn't complaining.

At lunchtime, she almost bumped into him coming out of the canteen. He seemed so keen to get away from her that it was almost hilarious.

He didn't go to fencing. Again, no complaints there.

"Where's Daniel?" asked Mr Boyd.

"He had to go home, Sir," said one of Danny's friends.

Well, that was good news. Another fencing lesson

without Danny. Cat threw herself into the lesson, lunging and parrying as though it was Danny she was fighting.

Oddly, though, the passion had gone out of it and, although she was pleased with the praise that came from Boyd, she found that she no longer particularly hated Danny.

Perhaps all that was over.

CHAPTER 30
FOLLOWED AGAIN

CAT was walking home from the bus stop after hockey. It was two days later, Hallowe'en and mint cold. Dusk was falling fast from a cloud-heavy sky and it was beginning to rain. Her dad had taken Angus into town for a full rehearsal for the concert and then he was going to see a friend before bringing Angus home afterwards. Then Angus would be going trick-or-treating, no doubt. Her mum was not allowed to drive yet. Cat's bike had still not been fixed and, anyway, with the extra darkness now that the clocks had gone back, she wasn't allowed to do an evening cycle ride till spring. Normally she'd have argued about this, but she'd let it go.

So Cat was going home on her own, though her dad would not be happy about it if he knew. He thought she was getting a lift, but it had turned out that there wasn't anyone who *could* give her a lift. She'd been going to ask Ailsa's mum but she was taking Ailsa and her sister to some aunt's house for tea and Cat didn't have the nerve to ask her to go completely in the wrong direction, even though she wouldn't have minded. And by then, the others had gone.

Anyway, her dad was overreacting. She'd been making her own way home from school for nearly two years now. It wasn't that far from the bus stop. And there'd be people around.

But now he suddenly seemed to want her to be collected or to promise to walk with other people. It was ridiculous. OK, so she knew he'd been upset by her mum's accident – who wouldn't be – but that didn't mean he had to see danger everywhere.

"Just do what you're told, Catriona, please. Humour me, OK?"

Ridiculous.

She made her way along the tree-lined road from the bus stop. A gust snatched at the branches, tumbling leaves adrift. The wet scrunch of her footsteps was loud in the evening air, though mixed with other noises: the swoosh of a car passing along the hospital road, the wind in her ears and in the branches. Gobbets of rain falling through the trees and hitting the car roofs. A siren from afar, and then another. A distant horn. Another car.

Some little kids came tottering round the corner dressed as ghosts and fairies – wet fairies with stomping feet – shepherded by two parents. One kid was crying and one was being carried, its sheet tangled round its wellies. Cat waited for them to pass. Their silly noise disappeared into the darkness.

She hurried on, her blazer collar hunched round her neck and her scarf wrapped round her head. Footsteps came from the side. A man with a dog. They passed by.

She crossed the road. A sudden noise like a snapping twig behind her made her turn. Nothing. She carried on, her heart beating faster, though she tried to stop it. Silly.

The door of some nearby flats opened and a man came out. He spent some time fumbling with his door, locking it. Looked in her direction, just briefly, in passing. Then walked round the corner until she could not see him.

She turned a corner and continued walking quickly homewards. She was nearly where her mum had had her accident, she realized. There was the lane, stretching into the gloom. A cat streaked across the end of it, low to the ground. The rain was unpleasant against her face and her hair would go curly. She hated that.

She passed parked cars, and a motorbike leaning on its support, a drenched cover over its seats.

Turned up the cobbled terrace. Darker here, no lights, few windows looking down. She could hear someone walking behind her. She looked round, but it must be someone still round the corner because she could see no one. And maybe she'd imagined it because now she could hear nothing other than the noises of normality. She began to jog, though carrying all her school stuff made it difficult. Now, she was in the next street to her own. Hers was just round one more corner. Nearly home.

A woman was getting into a car, waving goodbye to someone in a doorway before driving off. Leaving the street empty in the gathering gloaming. The door of that house closed tight.

But no, the street was not empty. A man was standing there, on the other side from her, beneath a broken streetlight. Just standing. A man in a thick padded coat, the hood up against the rain. He had a bicycle with him. He turned and saw her, and quickly wheeled his bicycle away, back out of the street. Which was odd because he'd looked as though he'd been about to go *into* the street. It wasn't anyone she recognized. Mind you, she hadn't seen his face and she couldn't tell much from what she had seen – just the coat and body shape. And the bike was just any bike, scruffy, old-fashioned, an old man's bike.

Nothing to do with her.

Whatever, she needed to get home. Fast.

She almost ran towards her own street, less unnerved now that she was so close to home. Turned the corner. With relief she saw her front door, the lights on upstairs. But she knew, with absolute certainty, that there were footsteps behind her. It could, of course, be coincidence, just someone also hurrying through the rain and cold. But what if it wasn't?

Mrs Morris came out of her front door and began to walk slowly towards the other end of the street, stopping to put something in her bin, and Cat realized that nothing bad could happen while Mrs Morris was within view. Cat could wait just inside her own front door and see if anyone came past. See who had been following her. If anyone. It was probably no one, or just someone quite innocently walking in the same direction. With danger passed, it suddenly felt unreal.

She tugged her bag off her shoulders, to find her key. Where was it? Mrs Morris had reached the end of the street and disappeared from view. The streetlight wasn't working near their house, which was not helping her find the key. She couldn't ring the doorbell as she didn't want to disturb her mum. And her dad and Angus wouldn't be back yet.

Where was her key? What if someone *was* following her? Where had the footsteps gone? She darted a glance back the way she'd come, towards the corner. Could she hear something? Was someone waiting there?

A sudden increase in the wind and rain battered her ears, drowning her ability to hear any other sounds.

Where was her key? There! She grasped it, fumbling with the lock, opened the door, shouted, "I'm home!" and the relief she felt was enormous. She could have laughed, except that the cold feeling still shrivelled the skin on the back of her neck. She shivered as she looked back where she'd come from.

Silence. No – something. The scrunching of grit underfoot. And then, from round the corner of the wall, hurrying into the shadowy street, a figure came towards her.

Danny.

CHAPTER 31
CONFESSION BY CANDLELIGHT

"DANNY!"

"Cat."

Cat stepped through the front door. Her mum called from upstairs. "That you, Catty? Are you OK?"

"Course I'm OK. I'll be up in a minute."

Now she turned to Danny, who was still standing on the doorstep.

"What are you doing here?"

"I was following you." His face stared out from under the dripping hood.

"Any *particular* reason?"

"I have to talk to you."

"No, Danny, I don't think so."

"I do. I have to talk to you. Please."

Maybe this sounded interesting. Was he going to tell her about Phiz? The flowers? Apologize for being a creep?

His eyes were serious. There was no jeering, no swagger in the way he looked at her. "Can I come in?"

She said nothing. She really didn't want him to come in. At all. But … he did look serious. Kind of pleading. And she would be able to ask for the truth. Because that's what she felt he was going to tell her. Otherwise why else would he be here?

"Please."

Nodding, she turned and let him go past her into the house. "OK, but this had better be good." She shut the door, took off her wet coat, hung it up. "Put your coat there."

She called up the stairs as they went through the hall. "Mum, it's OK – I've got a friend from school with me. Do you want a cup of tea?"

"Lovely! I'm parched."

Cat led Danny towards the kitchen.

"Is your mum OK?"

"She's fine. She's off work for a while. Concussion. And she's broken her wrist. Do you want some tea?" She started making it.

"If you are. Thanks. Does she know what happened? I heard she thought someone jumped out at her."

"We don't know. She hasn't remembered any details. Do you want biscuits or something?" Without waiting for his reply she took a packet from the cupboard. Then went to the fridge and got the milk out. She felt him watching her, but it didn't matter. Oddly. He was more uncomfortable than she was. "Milk? Sugar? Biscuit?

We'll take a tray to my mum and then we'll go to my room. If it's not too *princess* for you."

"I … I don't think…"

"What?"

"Nothing."

After a short silence while she finished making the three mugs of tea, he followed her towards the stairs. Then he spoke again. "Look, I don't want your mum to know I'm here."

"Why?"

"Please."

"But she knows nothing about you. She knows I went out with a Danny for a while but she doesn't even know your second name, I don't think."

"But she might."

"So what if she does?"

"It's important. Trust me. Please."

This was weird. Really weird. But then he always was. Weird insect boy. Why had she ever gone out with him?

"If you say so. Hold this." They were on the landing now. She gave Danny the tray and took a mug from it, before going into her parents' bedroom.

"Thanks, Catty. Lovely. You had a good day?" She was curled up on the sofa, wrapped in a rug, a book lying on the floor. Polly lay beside her, thwacking her tail on the carpet.

"Fine, thanks. You OK?"

"Kind of. Just tired. Dad fed Polly before he went

out with Angus, in case you're wondering why she didn't come and pester you in the kitchen."

"OK. Anyway, we'll be upstairs." She would have liked to stay and chat, tell her more, tell her properly, but…

She went back out onto the landing, where Danny was waiting.

"Come up then." And she led the way. He'd been in her room before, of course. When he'd made the princess remarks. Well, he could think what he liked. She didn't care.

When she switched on the light, the bulb went. "Damn!" Well, she wasn't going downstairs to get a bulb and, to be honest, darkness was preferable to bright light just now. She switched on her bedside lamp and lit some of the many candles in the fire-grate and on the mantelpiece. One she put on the window ledge, the shutters open. She didn't really need to light so many but the more she lit, the longer she put off whatever Danny was going to say. She did want to know, but she also didn't. Lighting candles was a lot easier.

She glanced out of the window, barely noticing the lights of other windows through the rain-streaked glass.

Cat sat on the bed, looking down. Danny sat cross-legged on the floor. She brushed her damp hair, straightening the rain-curled bits.

"So what is it you want to say?"

"I … well, I don't know… It's…" He hesitated.

"You're not making much sense, you know."

"I know." He was picking at the little bits of skin round his fingernails. She noticed that his hand seemed completely healed. He wasn't looking at her. There was a smell of wet clothes, unpleasant.

"It's about my brother."

"Your *brother*? I didn't even know you had one."

"He's older than me. Much older. He left home ages ago. He's ... ill. He dropped out. Cannabis and stuff. Actually, he was expelled, if you must know. Mum and Dad tried to help him, but now..." Danny turned away, but not before she'd seen his mouth tremble. This was embarrassing. The darkness and flickering lights made everything even more unreal.

"What, Danny?"

"He has schizophrenia."

CHAPTER 32
MADNESS

THE word smashed into her mind, shocking in the half-dark. Shocking anywhere. A terrible word.

Danny continued. "But he takes pills that work really well." He looked at her, his face bright. "He isn't locked away or anything – he's not that bad. We have an uncle who lives near here and David is staying with him. My parents aren't coping well but our uncle is not so close, not as … I don't know, not as sad. It makes Mum and Dad really cut up to see David. It's horrible then."

Cat didn't know what to say. Something choked inside her. What would it be like to have a brother like that? What would that do to her parents?

"Look, Danny, I'm sorry about your brother but … what has this got to do with me?"

"He's not dangerous, honestly. He wouldn't do anything. He's never hurt anyone. You hear about schizophrenics hurting people, but his pills are really good. And Uncle Walter makes sure he takes them."

"Danny, just a minute – what's this got to do with me?"

"Because of Phiz. I think it was him."

"What?" She stared at him. It took a few seconds for her to work out what he meant. "Your brother was the spider guy on Phiz? God, that's totally creepy! I had a schizophrenic watching me on the internet? Sorry," she added when she saw his face.

"And how do you know about the Phiz stuff anyway?" she asked.

"After you said that thing at fencing, I asked around and one of my friends had heard one of your friends talking about it."

Great. So everyone knew. "But why would your brother do that?"

"Because of us."

"Us?"

"I was so angry. When you dumped me. Well, you treated me like rubbish, didn't you?"

"Yeah. Sorry. But you weren't exactly perfect yourself. You grossed me out with your insects, you slagged me off for having more money than you, you… Look, OK, I'm sorry. OK? I am. I know the way I did it wasn't great."

"No, it wasn't. But yeah, I'm sorry too. Anyway, the point is I was mad at you. And I told David all about it. He wasn't ill then. This was months ago. He was great. I'm sorry, but we used to have 'Let's slag Cat off again' sessions. Come on!" he said when he saw her about to speak. "I bet you do the same with your friends."

She was silent.

"Anyway, then he got ill. It happened quite suddenly, though Mum and Dad said there were signs earlier. And he started obsessing about what a cow you were. He was way over the top in some of the things he said. My uncle helped calm him down. But he was still ill. Then when I heard someone was doing that to you on Phiz, I guessed it was him. I asked him and he denied it, but I didn't believe him. It's obvious, isn't it? He'd been talking about getting back at you. But actually I didn't think it would do any harm. All he could do was scare you. And that was fine by me – I was still mad at you. So I left it."

"So he knew all the details about me because you'd told him?"

"Sorry. But if you think about it, the details are on your open profile anyway. Your hobbies and everything. Not exactly a secret, is it? That's why I don't do that stuff."

"Where did all this happen? What computer did he use? Does he have his own?"

"No, he can't afford one. Or maybe he uses Uncle Walter's when he's round there."

"So this uncle knows all about me too, does he? Really great."

"Sorry. But he's OK, really. I wouldn't talk to Mum and Dad about that stuff, but he's OK. They don't get on with Uncle Walter but even they're glad he's helping David. I'm not really supposed to go round there as much as I do, but Uncle Walter's interesting. And now David's there, there's even more reason … he's my brother."

"Listen, your brother may be ill and I obviously feel sorry for him and all that, but do you realize what he's done? He wrecked my computer with a virus for a start. I lost a whole load of work and he freaked me out."

"You'll think this is mad but this stuff has been going round my head – ever since your mum fell off her bike near the psych hospital and I heard maybe someone had jumped out at her. People started talking about how it might have been a mental patient and I just … freaked. He'd been chucked out of the hospital that day. It could have been him! It's really stupid because I know David wouldn't do anything like—"

"*How* do you know? Don't people with schizophrenia have voices that make them do things?" Cat didn't know what to think. It was a horrible idea, really horrible, to think that David – or anyone – might have attacked her mum. On purpose. Her mum had almost managed to convince herself that she'd been imagining that someone jumped out at her; it had been too weird, too horrible to believe. Better to believe it was an accident. But now…

Danny was talking. "I don't know. I don't know what to do. I'm really worried it might have been him but if I say something and it's not… It would wreck him to be questioned by the police and how would he prove he was innocent? It could end up being a real mess and it would be my fault."

"Have you told your mum and dad?"

"No. I wanted to, but I bottled it. They've been worried enough about him already. We don't know anyone was involved, do we? I mean all that stuff at school about being attacked by ... by a mentally ill person, that was just rumour. But I hated it, Cat. It really scared me."

"And you didn't come into school."

"No, I couldn't. I said I was ill."

He still picked at his fingers.

"Stop doing that, Danny."

He looked up. "Sorry."

"Stop saying… Oh, forget it."

They sat without speaking, while the rain hurled itself against the window, the thin claws of branches scraping on the glass. In the draught, the candles swayed.

A sudden thought hit her. The accident: her mum had been riding her bike, wearing *her* helmet, and in the place where Cat would normally have been at more or less that time. She'd already thought that it *could* easily have been her instead. But what if it was *meant* to be her instead?

It was possible: Danny's brother, a mental patient, was apparently out to get her. She felt cold. Her thoughts were tangled, leading nowhere.

And, she realized, with horror, her timetable had been on Phiz until recently. David would know she cycled after hockey, would perhaps have watched her before, but would not have known that on this occasion it would be her mum and not her.

Not sure if she should say anything or not, she hesitated. Struggled to find the right words to express such an absurd fear. When she did find the words, she could see the fear reflected in Danny's eyes.

"No! He wouldn't! He couldn't!"

"How do you know? You can't be sure."

"We *have* to go and see my uncle. He'll know what to do. He looks after David – he might even have been with him that evening. He must have been. That was the day David was discharged from the hospital! He *was* with my uncle."

Cat didn't know what to think. She wished her dad was home. She peered at her watch. No, he'd be ages yet.

Danny continued. "We should go and see him, Cat. Ask him. Please! I need to know."

"But what if we meet your brother?"

"I'll be there and so will my uncle. There's nothing to be worried about. I'm sure David didn't do it but, please, Cat. I feel … bad. I really need to know."

This couldn't be happening. Stuff like this just didn't happen, not in real life. She should get a grip. There was no real evidence that anyone had attacked her mum – she'd probably just fallen off her bike, knocked askew by a pothole or loose stone or something. Even faulty brakes would be better than this.

"No, let's wait for my dad. You can stay here till he comes back with Angus. Why don't you phone your parents and tell them where you are?"

"I'm supposed to be at a friend's house doing homework anyway, so they won't be worrying. I need to talk to Uncle Walter, Cat. He's the only person who will know what to do."

Cat could think of few things she would like to do less. She had absolutely no desire to see Danny's Uncle Walter. He knew things about her and none of it good. On the other hand, she didn't trust Danny to sort it out entirely himself. She wanted to know as well. And if she was with Danny, she'd be safe. There was a weird thought!

"Help me blow the candles out." And they did. Downstairs, Cat went into her parents' room. Her mum was sleeping. Cat wished she could tell her everything. But there was just too much to explain. And anyway, nothing bad could come just from going to talk to Danny's uncle. Maybe he *could* reassure them. If he had been with Danny's brother all that evening, that would be that.

One thing she knew for certain – if she still had doubts after she'd spoken to him, she would tell her parents everything. Just thinking that made her feel better.

There could be no harm in delaying for an hour, she told herself.

She shook her mum's shoulder gently. "Mum, I'm just going round to my friend's house, OK?"

"Whose house?"

"Friend from school – we've got a bit of homework to finish."

It worked every time, thought Cat, as her mum murmured agreement.

After texting her dad to say she'd gone to a friend's house and would be back soon, Cat went out of the house with Danny. They left plenty of lights on, and Polly asleep in her bed downstairs, dreaming of a world full of cats, rabbits and squirrels and a warm fire to lie beside afterwards.

Wrapped up against the sheeting rain, they hurried along the street, round the corner and into the next street, past some more stupid ghosts, pumpkins and fairies, and one white rabbit in tears, down the cobbled road, and in a couple of minutes came to the building where Danny said his uncle lived.

As they stood in the slight shelter of the doorway, and waited for his voice to answer the intercom, Cat looked up. It was an old building, originally one enormous house but now divided into flats. Its huge square tower at one end made it one of the tallest buildings around, and the view from the windows up there must be spectacular. Soon a metallic voice came through the grid: "Yes?"

"It's Danny. Can I come up?" A pause. A long pause.

Then the buzz of the door and Danny pushed it open. "Come on!"

"I don't like this, Danny." Cat felt distinctly uncomfortable.

"Don't be silly. It's going to be fine. Uncle Walter will sort everything. He'll know what to do."

Cat knew what she wanted to do: run back home and curl up in her room, safe with her mum and dog, and wait for her dad and Angus to come back. Nothing could harm her there. But here, about to go up the stairs to a strange man who knew all sorts of things about her? Not the most fun-sounding suggestion of the year.

She vowed to stay for ten minutes only. Then she'd go back home and tell her mum. Everything.

She wished her friends were here. They wouldn't know any better than her what to do but they could at least do it together. She had a real urge to text them … but to say what? That she was with Danny, about to go into his uncle's flat to ask questions about his schizophrenic brother? To find out if he'd tried to kill her? Completely stupid idea.

Trust Danny to get her into this. Never trust someone who collects insects.

She stepped into the building. There was a bicycle leaning against the wall of the vestibule. Wet footprints staining the floor. A smell of petrol. And, hanging from a hook, a motorbike tarpaulin.

Danny pushed open a door on the left and she looked up the staircase, hesitated, and followed him up the stairs.

CHAPTER 33
THE WATCHER
NOW: HALLOWE'EN

HE is private and warm in his room, at his desk overlooking the surrounding streets. The rain slides, slanting across the large windowpanes, and the wind drags the branches of the trees in a crazy dance.

He likes being alone. There have been times in his life when too many people have been around him. He avoids groups where possible. Most people worry about too much and too little – they have no idea of reality. He has seen things to turn the mind and the stomach, things that most people see only in films or nightmares. He has seen war.

Everything is coming together now. His fingers are tired, as they rattle across the keys of his computer. His book is well on its way. The book is about his experiences. It *has* made him feel much better. Cathartic, people say it is, to write unbearable memories down. And it has been. Though the act of finding the words to convey the raw and terrible events has been painful. But each time a little less so.

Now he can write almost without crying.

The notebook with its thick paper lies beside him, full of circles and plans, mind maps and links and question marks, though with almost all the question marks at last crossed out.

He has interest from a publisher. Though he does not wish for fame or fortune. Wealth is wicked and all property is theft. He is not writing this for money, but for himself. And for all his friends who died while he lived. Often when he closes his eyes, he sees them, sees their throats split as if screaming through shrapnel and the sharp flames of gunfire. He smells acid smoke and tastes vomit. Oddly, the taste of grapefruit is at the back of his throat too. He does not know why. It is bitter and thin and nasty and should not be there.

When Walter had discovered, weeks ago, that his own nephew had actually been going out with the daughter of Dr Bill McPherson, that had been a shocking moment. He had almost knocked on the man's door and shouted his pent-up anger at him. But where would that have got him? This was not supposed to be about Bill McPherson.

But it has been impossible not to watch the house, not while writing these memoirs, not when every time he looks up from his desk he sees the shiny black door. There are now too many reasons to watch.

Before Walter went off to the First Gulf War, he and his wife had been happy. He'd come back home in

1991. Victorious. Well, 358 Allied deaths and countless thousands of Iraqis. Sounded like a victory, didn't it? If measured like that.

But two of the deaths had been Walter's closest friends. He'd seen them die. And so had Bill McPherson, the doctor on duty when the casualties were brought in, their wounds too horrific to describe. Doctor, yes; professional soldier, no. Just one of those part-timers, Territorial Army, joined for the action and excitement and never expected to be called up for real war.

Walter, his right hand shielding the hole in one man's skull, the left hand gripped painfully in the dying man's fist, had yelled at him to do something. But the doctor had refused, his face passive. "In a minute," he'd said. Busy, he'd said he was. Busy. With an officer and a mangled arm. So Walter's friend had died, with Walter's hand still sticky where the skull had been. And the other hand painful long after the dying grip had vanished. With his other friend simply moaning more and more quietly until the moan disappeared altogether and Walter realized that he was dead too, while nurses and doctors bustled round in the heat and dust, doing their best, and Bill McPherson focused on the one soldier whose arm he was trying to save.

In Walter's grief, people had told him that he was in shock and being unreasonable, that Bill McPherson had only done what he must do – save the life he was working on before any others that came in after, and that a gaping head wound was a hopeless case. But Walter had been the one with his hand on that wound. He'd been the one who watched his friend's glazed eyes as he slipped away.

When "victory" had come, and Walter had found himself standing mute on a British harbourside some months later, his wife running towards him, he had felt numb. Had not been able to put his arms round her, kiss her, tell her he loved her. Because he didn't, not any more. How could you? How could you go from death and pain and hate and fear to a woman's warm perfume?

Despite this, and the rows, the anger, his silent evenings staring at a whisky bottle, his wife had become pregnant, maybe a year later. She'd told him straightaway, looking at him with frightened, hopeful eyes as though she dreamed that this might change everything. Out of death, might come life. Out of horror, could come pastel love and warm milk and baby clothes.

It hadn't. Things had got worse. Trapped and guilty, he felt by then. And he had been cruel to Sheila, he knew that. Knew it even at the time, but could not bite his tongue and stop the acid words before they were said.

And when the baby – a girl – had been stillborn a few months later, how could Sheila not have blamed him? How could everyone not have blamed him? After all, he'd blamed himself.

His daughter would have been Cat's age now. And that was the problem. Not his, but Sheila's. Her grief had never entirely gone away. In many ways, she had coped unbelievably well. When he'd left her, disappearing one sad sunny day two months later and leaving only a gutless handwritten note, she'd been helped by friends – including his sister, Danny and David's mother. And eventually, eventually, she had come through her grief, got herself together and gone back to work. Computers. Brilliant, she was. But she'd changed.

She no longer wanted to be near people. Now she lived alone, a strangely simple life. But that summer, she'd been talking to Danny – always had a soft spot for him, she did – and, to cut a long story short, she'd realized that Danny had been going out with the daughter of Bill McPherson, a man her husband had often talked of when drunk and angry or when he woke screaming and sobbing from a nightmare. And she'd seen Cat one day, seen her glowing health and, frankly, beauty, and realized that Bill McPherson had the daughter she should have had, while she had no one.

So she'd gone off the rails. Not mad. Because it wasn't really mad, was it? It was totally, utterly sane and reasonable to feel jealous and hurt and angry and sad. Nothing mad about that.

But he worries about her, and what she might do in her fury. Things she's been saying seem ... over the top. The way she watches the house: he's seen her from his window. So now he sometimes finds himself watching the girl, sometimes even following her on his bike. If he knows that Sheila is following, then Walter will too, to keep an eye on her.

And now he has David to worry about too, poor lad.

There's real madness.

But where is David? He should be here. Walter has agreed to keep him with him at all times. He has seemed much better. And this evening Walter has let him go to buy beans or something. There had not seemed any harm in that. He'd gone on his motorbike, and there was no reason why he shouldn't.

Come on, David! Walter is irritated. He wants to get on with his writing. And David's absence is stopping him. Not that he is worried, but until David is settled down in his own room, with the endless DVDs he watches, Walter cannot immerse himself in his work.

He looks out of the window. Most of the leaves have gone now. He can see the street where the McPhersons live, see the girl's window, see the lights on behind shutters and curtains, see her own light on with no shutters. Suddenly the light goes off, and he sees her face bend down to blow out a candle which is burning on her windowsill.

He has no warm feelings for her. She hurt his younger nephew with her cruel behaviour. She looks spoilt, with that thick rich hair and that expensive house. But he does not exactly hate her. She's only a girl, a kid.

He doesn't like people like her, though. People who always have so much more than they need. His nose wrinkles in contempt for such greed.

He turns away from his window.

Where is David? What is he doing?

Walter calms himself by looking at his new insect, the

one that had arrived only that day. He has not written the card for it yet. It is the one that Danny helped him choose recently.

He looks at the insect for a few moments, feeling his tension ease. David will come back. He will be fine. Sheila will calm down again. Everything will work out.

The creature is extraordinary. It is green and smooth. And, when alive, moves slowly. It has the amazing ability to turn its head completely round, and to look behind itself. The eyes point forward, allowing it to see like humans. If it was alive.

And so, flexing the fingers of his left hand, always stiff in cold weather ever since the war – not that he specifically injured it, just that ever since the day his friend gripped him as he died, his hand has felt different, cold, cramped, as though the blood goes to it only when forced – he holds down the waiting card and begins to write, in slow, well formed letters: Mantodea – *Choeradodis stalii*. And he blows the ink dry before placing it next to the insect sitting waiting in its clear plastic box.

He smiles.

The doorbell rings. David. At last!

He goes to the intercom. "David?"

"It's Danny. Can I come up?" Danny! Danny was becoming annoying. He was always worrying about David. His parents should be the ones to listen to his problems, or his friends. Didn't he realize his uncle was busy? He must have a word with Danny's mother, Walter's sister. Not that she would welcome his call. She didn't like the way he was getting too close to David and Danny. She and Walter had never got on. Well, she'd let one son go off the rails – not surprising if she felt she'd failed and was screwed up by guilt. She was always so judgemental. But what did she know about the real world? Cushioned, she was. What he'd seen in the Gulf was unspeakably terrible. But even though Iraq had damaged him, it had given him his edge, had made him human. He knew what being alive meant because he knew what death meant.

He said nothing but pressed the buzzer and waited for the boy to reach the top of the stairs.

CHAPTER 34
FACE TO FACE

THE door opened and a dim light pooled across the landing. Cat could see the man silhouetted in the doorway, his face in darkness.

"Hi," said Danny. "I've brought Cat. We need to talk to you."

"I'm pretty busy, actually, Danny. You should have told me you were coming. You can come in, of course, but I can't talk for long. And shouldn't you be at home? Doing homework or something?"

"Sorry," said Danny, looking uncomfortable. "Is David here?"

"No. He's gone out to get something from Waitrose. He'll be back soon."

"Is that…"

"Don't worry, Danny. He's fine. He's not a prisoner. Anyway, what can I do for you? Both. Come in and sit down. Do you want some biscuits or anything? Coffee?

Juice?" And he looked at Cat, straight at her eyes. She could not tell at all what he was thinking. She looked away. He made her feel uncomfortable: the idea that he knew so much about her, and probably disapproved of her already, was hard to take.

There was something familiar about him, she realized. It could be that she'd seen him around locally, but it felt like more than that.

His hair was greasy. Or wet. Yes, wet – he'd probably been out in the rain. His face, well, it was sort of ordinary. Bit like Mr Turner's in some ways: tight, hard. Really short hair.

"No, thanks," said Danny. Cat shook her head too.

"Well, I need coffee myself so I'll be a minute or two. Sit down while you're waiting."

They followed him into his sitting room and he went through another door, presumably to his kitchen. The two of them sat on a sofa and waited. Danny fiddled with his phone. Cat looked round. The man had been doing something on his computer – the screensaver was floating around. A notebook lay open by the keyboard, full of scribbles.

"What does your uncle do?" she whispered to Danny.

"He's a security guy for a financial company. But he's writing his memoirs now. He was a soldier. It's weird – he doesn't actually talk about it. I've sometimes tried to get him to tell me stuff about it, but he won't. And now he's writing it all down. I think it's because of what's going on in Iraq – he was in the First Gulf War."

"So was my dad."

"Seriously? He was in the army?"

"Territorial Army. He went as a doctor. He doesn't talk about it much either. To be honest, I don't really ask. I don't think I want to know."

"I want to know. We *should* know. If we don't know what happens in war then how will our generation do anything about it when it's our turn to make decisions?"

Cat looked at him. Serious stuff. He sounded … what? Strong. Fired up.

"I want to go into politics," he said, simply.

Cat didn't know what to say. Not just an insect boy then.

He went on, almost whispering, looking quickly at the door to the kitchen. "My mum says he was wrecked by the war. She never forgave him for how he behaved when he came back. He was married to a friend of hers. She won't give details but I think he was pretty horrible to his wife."

The door handle turned. Danny's uncle was coming back in, with a mug of coffee. He looked at his watch.

She still couldn't work out where she'd seen him.

"So what did you want to talk about, Danny?" The wind moaned in the chimney.

Danny hesitated. "It's about David."

His uncle looked at Cat, frowning a little.

"She knows about his illness," said Danny.

"David needs support. He doesn't need you undermining him."

Danny carried on, though his face was flushed. Cat couldn't help respecting him a bit, just carrying on talking while his uncle was being so, well, rude. "Thing is, Cat's mother had an accident last week, fell off her bike. Well, I know this sounds stupid but I thought it could have been David that caused it. Sort of by mistake. Thinking it was Cat. You know how he was about her a few weeks ago, when … well, you know. Anyway, Cat thought that maybe…"

Uncle Walter turned towards her, his face without expression. "You thought what?"

Cat knew this had been a bad idea. It was going to sound so stupid.

"Look, I don't mean to be … sort of … horrible, but what with the stuff on Phiz and then what Danny said about his brother hating me and then my mum's accident when I should…"

"Phiz?"

"It's a networking site. You…"

"I know what Phiz is," he said. "What's it got to do with this?"

Cat looked at Danny.

He spoke. "Cat had someone watching her on Phiz and hassling her and whoever it was put a virus into her laptop."

"And you think that was David?" He looked at both of them.

"I thought it was," said Danny. "It could be. I know he's better now but then…"

"And where do you think he would have done that? He doesn't have a computer."

"I thought … he used yours?"

"No, he doesn't. He's not interested. He watches DVDs. I would let him use mine, but he's never asked and he doesn't like internet cafés – too many people. And before you ask: my computer is password protected. So don't go suspecting your brother of everything, just because he's ill."

"But he said something once, ages ago, about how I should use Phiz to get my own back on Cat." Cat looked at Danny. He hadn't said that before.

"But you didn't, did you? And he didn't either."

"Could he have used a computer in the hospital?" asked Cat.

"I don't think they're very likely to let patients have internet access, are they?" He stared back at each of them in turn. Cat didn't like his eyes. He was flexing the fingers of his left hand, massaging them. "And wasn't there something else you wanted to know?"

They looked at him. He stared at Cat.

"Your mother's accident? You thought my nephew could have been involved." He managed to sneer so slightly that it was hardly perceptible.

"I…" She didn't know what to say. Yes, she did want to know, but he had managed to make her feel so small that she couldn't ask.

But he was continuing. "What day did it happen? What time?"

"Friday. Last Friday. About six thirty. In the evening."

He got up and went over to his desk. Picked up a notebook, diary of some sort, flicked back a page. Only the wind and rain made any noise as they waited.

"That was the day David was discharged – against his will, I may add – and I agreed to take him. He was with me all evening. And it wasn't exactly what I wanted either. It's quite a responsibility, you know," and at this he looked at Cat. She looked away. Towards the window.

Beside the window was a noticeboard, a pinboard thing. Her eyes were caught by something familiar. A season ticket for the swimming pool. The fitness centre where she trained.

And then she knew where she had seen him. He was the guy at the fitness centre, who had complimented her on her swimming. And who'd seen her club tracksuit and kitbag.

She looked back at him. He was staring at her and, before she could say anything, he spoke. His face quite different. The friendly uncle all of a sudden.

"I've seen you before, haven't I? At the swimming pool. Anyway, I'm Danny's uncle. As you now know. Pleased to meet you, at last." The sarcasm suited him.

She mumbled something in return. A feeling of nervousness came over her and she really wanted to leave.

At any moment David could come back from wherever he was. She didn't like the sound of him, even if he hadn't been responsible for her mum's accident, or Phiz, and she didn't like Danny's uncle. But if David couldn't have harmed her mum then there was no need for her to be here now. And she wanted to get home. Suddenly she really wanted that, just to be safe at home.

But now the uncle turned to Danny. "It arrived, you know? Do you want to see it?"

Danny looked at Cat. He seemed … embarrassed? His uncle was picking something up from the table beside his desk. A plastic box. And then she knew.

Another insect collector. The uncle was weird too! She'd been right. Inside, she almost laughed. There was obviously a secret underworld of mad, creepy insect collectors, all comparing the merits of their disgusting creatures.

"Come on – you chose it for me. Great choice, Danny! A real beauty!" Uncle Walter was smiling, the skin of his cheeks creased like corrugated cardboard.

He brought the box towards them. Now she really wanted to get out of there.

"I should be getting back, Danny. My mum might need something."

Uncle Walter ignored her excuse. "Look! Nothing to be afraid of. Just a dead insect. I know you don't like living ones – hissing cockroaches, for example." He knew about that? She glared at Danny, who was not looking at her. "But this one is different:

Mantodea: – *Choeradodis stalii*, commonly called the Praying Mantis."

"I'm not afraid, actually. But I should be getting back." Danny and his uncle weren't listening. Danny put his phone down.

The insect was green. Smooth. It looked like a toy, something you'd buy after a visit to a natural history museum. It was quite beautiful in a way, and not at all hairy. So when he held it out for her to take the box, she did. Just like that. She quelled the rush of adrenalin, stopped her hand shaking, and just held the box in front of her, turning it this way and that. And then she passed it to Danny.

She kept her fear inside. She would not let the man see it.

CHAPTER 35
CHASED BY FEAR ITSELF

"DANNY, I've really got to go now."

"Yes, Danny. You should be getting back home as well, shouldn't you? And I need to get back to my work."

Cat and Danny both stood up. Put their wet coats back on. Uncle Walter watched them.

She wanted to get out before the crazy brother came back. Even if he was on his pills. Even if he'd been tucked up safely with a mug of herbal tea watching a DVD of *Shrek* when her mum had her accident. She could ask her mother about him. Probably she wouldn't get any details – patient confidentiality and all that – but her mother could at least reassure her.

Uncle Walter saw them to the bottom of the stairs. Closed the inner door behind them as they left.

It was raining harder as they went through the outer door and it clunked shut. Cat pulled her hood up and began to run, barely waiting to see if Danny was following, though she could hear that he was.

Cat couldn't explain the fear that gripped her now. It was like that feeling you get in dreams. When something is following, and it's getting closer. Your back crawls as though cold fingers are about to clutch it. Your legs are too heavy for running.

But she did run, Danny following, down the path and onto the street, along the pavement to the end, through slithery mess of leaves, across, round the corner, up the cobbled road, into the street next to hers.

What was she afraid of? Probably nothing, if she'd stopped to think. But Uncle Walter and the thought of schizophrenic David, and the darkness itself, had all come together to make her want nothing more than to be home, safe indoors in the warm. And the faster she ran, the more afraid she felt, until she wanted to scream.

It was hard to hear anything above the rain drumming on car roofs, the wind in the trees and the sound of her own breathing. There was the street in front of her, sliding round the corner into further darkness.

"Wait!" Danny was shouting behind her.

She stopped and turned, breathing heavily, holding her hand up to shield her eyes from the rain. "What?"

"I've got to go back!"

"Why?" she yelled.

"I left my phone."

Cat's language was not what her parents would have liked. But she certainly wasn't going back with him.

Why should she? It was *his* uncle. *His* phone. *His* sick brother. They were nothing to do with her.

Besides, he wasn't a baby; it was early evening, not night-time; and he was only a few minutes from his home. On residential streets. She didn't have to accompany him. And she was home already. Or almost.

"Look, Danny, we'll talk later but I've had enough of this. You have to tell your mum and dad if you're worried about David."

"Listen, Cat, I'm sorry, OK? And thanks too – for not getting mad with me."

"Yeah, well. Can I go home now? I'm soaking wet. You can call round if you want. Later this evening. Or text me when you get home or something. OK?" She meant it, she realized. It wasn't just that she felt sorry for him about David. But they had shared stuff. There were things he knew that others didn't. She wanted to tell her friends but for some reason that would have felt wrong – Danny's brother was mentally ill and maybe he didn't want other people to know. OK, so she hadn't owed him anything before, but he'd been honest with her. Maybe Danny was the only person she could talk to about this.

She ran round the corner. The sound of his footsteps went in the other direction.

Relief flooded through her as she arrived in her own street, saw her own shiny black door.

Better still, the outer door was open; her dad and Angus must be back early. Very early. Well, she'd find out why soon. She went in. The hall was in complete darkness. She fumbled for the switch in the porch. Nothing. Not another power cut? They must have only just got back and her dad would be finding the candles now. She unbuttoned her coat, but kept it on, planning to put it in the airing cupboard. Shook rain from her hair. Left the outer door open to let in some streetlight.

Only later did she wonder why the streetlight was on if it was a power cut.

She picked up the torch from its place. Faintly wondered why it was there if her dad had taken it through to the kitchen. Opened the inner door and swung the beam round the hall.

Shouted up the stairs, "Hello! I'm back!" Took in the silence, was briefly puzzled.

"Hello? Where are you?"

Nothing. Now fear clutched at her, though she could not say why. She took a few steps forward. Where was Polly? The door in front of her was closed. It was normally open. Maybe her mother had shut it. But where *was* her mum? Asleep upstairs? "Mum?"

She was sure she'd heard something. She whipped round, the torch beam careering over the ceiling. And that was when she heard another noise. The front door closing. She screamed as a figure loomed from the darkness by the door.

CHAPTER 36
CAUGHT

NOW a much stronger torch beam shone straight at her eyes, painfully. Cat could see nothing of who was behind it. A quiet voice snarled, "Shut up! I have a knife. Scream again and I'll use it."

She could hear Polly scratching on the other side of the dining-room door. And then barking.

The figure pushed past Cat, opened the door where Polly was, and snapped, "Shut it!" Polly barked again. The door slammed hard and there was a yelp. Cat cringed and a sob of fear rose in her throat. The man turned his attention to Cat.

"Don't think about fighting. You want to see the knife?" As soon as she heard the voice again, she realized, confused, that this wasn't a man – it was a woman.

But the knife, held up in the torchlight, was terrifying whoever held it. Sickeningly fat, tapering quickly to a sharp point, it was not the sort of knife Cat had ever seen in a kitchen.

The woman's next words were said in a voice so flat, so soft, that Cat struggled to make sense of their cruelty. "And then even your daddy's skills won't save you."

Cat felt her arm grabbed, fingers like talons pinching her flesh. She was propelled towards the front door. The woman opened it slightly, peering out while shining the torch in Cat's face, blinding her. Pulling her out of the door, the woman shut it behind them, and pushed her forward. A motorbike leaned against the fence, half hidden by the bins. Cat's vision was still blotched from the torch and she struggled to see in the dark.

A helmet was pushed onto her head. "Put it on – you'll need it. Then get on the bike." Fumbling, she managed to fasten the strap. Why was there no one around? There were people in houses close by: she should scream. She wanted to but she couldn't even breathe properly. And there was the knife. The idea of its slim point pressed against her side, slicing into her, was so horrible that she could only do what she was told. She climbed onto the seat.

The woman jumped on in front, switched the engine on and slammed it into gear. Where was the knife? Cat knew it must be somewhere. The bike lurched forward with a roar. Cat grabbed the woman. Could she jump off now? But everything was happening too fast. The thought of landing at speed on the road was too … horrible. She couldn't do it. In a few seconds, they'd have to slow before turning the corner. Could she…? No! The moment had passed. Too late. Fear paralysed her.

Left onto the main road, speeding down the hill, over the pedestrian lights. Cat shut her eyes as she was swept away from everything safe.

All she could do was hold on, gripping the thick leather jacket of her abductor, burying her face in its animal smell. Her fear was so terrible that she had no words for it, no thoughts other than the need to scream.

At some point they turned sharp right, and she leant precariously with the woman. She heard the angry hooting of horns. If they'd gone across a red light, maybe the police would have seen. Maybe someone would report them.

She forced her eyes open – she must see where they were going. They hurtled down a hill, across a junction and then up a steep hill. The bridge over the canal. Skidded almost to a halt. The woman steered deftly onto the footpath and within seconds they were by the canal. The woman jumped down and pulled her passenger off. Cat's legs crumpled, weak from gripping the seat. She was hauled roughly to her feet. The woman took her helmet off and gestured to Cat to do the same. She did, relieved to be rid of it.

Through the wet darkness, she saw someone approaching – a man with a dog. Her heart leapt: surely he would notice that she was not going willingly?

But she felt the horrible point of the knife at her side and heard the whisper, "Say nothing. One wrong sound and that'll be it. You've got more to lose than me." And the dog-walker turned off the path and went in the other direction.

Foul weather had kept everyone else inside. Scudding clouds across a thick sky meant no moonlight. And there were few lights at this part of the canal, though Cat could see the murky water well enough.

She wished she could shrink away to nothing, become invisible, wake up from the nightmare. Fear drenched each part of her, skin, blood, the roots of every hair. It clogged her breathing. Sapped her ability to think. She could die here. Somehow. She did not know how or why. Who would find her? What would it be like to...

The need to scream was welling up inside her – but that knife at her side kept her silent. And a bubble of fear clogged her throat.

Cat tried not to look at the foul silty water. At a mooring place, sat a houseboat. Cat recognized it: it belonged to the woman who'd given a crisp to Polly. Her brain was slow to understand. Until, suddenly, she did. This *was* that woman. But why, and what this meant, she could not imagine.

The woman took Cat's helmet. "Jump!" she instructed, with the knife still in her hand. Cat obeyed, grasping the rail. The woman then threw the helmets onto a coiled rope on the deck and unhooked a small ramp from the side of the houseboat. Cat should have done something then, jumped into the water, leapt at the woman while her hands were full – anything. But the sight of the knife took away all her courage and strength – her power to think or act.

She watched dully as the woman wheeled the bike up the ramp, leaving it occupying most of the deck. There was another narrow ramp that the woman must use when she put the bike on the low cabin roof, but she did not do this now. The flowers on the top of the cabin were dead. An old discoloured saucepan sat there, and a plastic petrol container where the motorbike had been. All this, Cat vaguely noticed as she waited, powerless as a frightened rabbit.

The woman unlocked a small door, opened it and pushed Cat in, so that she fell down two steps into the cabin. A smell of dead cigarette smoke hit her. And flowers, Cat knew the smell: lilies. Her mum was paranoid about the pollen staining things, always insisted on cutting the middle bits out. Stamens. The word came bizarrely to her. There was barely room to stand, and little surrounding space, though more than there had seemed to be from outside. Closed curtains and shutters kept the cabin cave-like. A sallow light from the canal path came through the door but otherwise all was dark.

The woman had cast off the rope now and scrambled into the cabin, pulling the door behind her, forcing her way past Cat and pushing open another door at the far end, the back of the boat, where she could dimly see a wheel and a few dials. Cat saw her turning something and then there was a jarring rattle as the engine started up and the houseboat began to move. A dim electric light hung by the woman's head, as she stood controlling the vessel. Cat could make out a little more of her surroundings: a bed further along, and the shadows of items, a box or trunk of some sort. And a vase on the table – lilies, huge, too big for the space. She felt the boat moving sluggishly, then picking up some speed.

Unreality merged with real, gut-churning fear. Cat struggled to control her thoughts. She should rush the woman. Hit her on the head with something. But no, the woman could see Cat. And she still had the knife. Even if Cat tried to escape through the door they'd come through, the woman could throw the knife. The very thought of it was paralysing. It made her almost sick. She swallowed. Her tongue stuck to the roof of her mouth.

She shivered, with cold, damp and terror. Her mum … there'd been no sound in the house. What if…?

There must be something she could do. Her phone. Could she send a text without looking at it? Coat pocket. Slowly, very slowly, she moved her hand towards it.

The woman shouted through the open door. "Looking for your phone?"

"No. I haven't … I don't…"

"Liar. Throw it here."

Cat hesitated.

"Do it! Fast! I'm counting. One … two…"

CHAPTER 37
CONVERSATION

CAT did as she was told, sliding the phone along the floor towards the open door. There were two missed calls, she could see.

"Now sit down and shut up." The woman left the phone there, only inches from where she stood.

Cat's body, colder now, began to shiver. It started with her leg, an uncontrollable shaking of one knee. And then, as she tried to tense her muscles against it, her whole body started to judder. Tears were not far away. She tried to breathe deeply, to tell herself that something would happen to save her. That if the woman wanted to kill her, surely she'd have done it by now. And as long as she didn't kill her, she could cope with anything. *Just don't kill me, please don't kill me, please don't kill me,* she silently prayed. She longed for her own house, her family. As she thought of them, the tears came closer.

Damp was seeping through her clothes, cold on her skin.

Time disappeared as the boat chugged along the canal. It could have been half an hour, or less, or more – ten minutes or forty – before she felt the vessel slow down. She looked through the far door, past the woman's head. It seemed much darker here. Where were they? Why hadn't she kept concentrating? If she'd been looking out properly she could have worked out where they were.

She must keep her wits about her, look for any chance to escape. Breathe, control, breathe. Somehow, she would get through this.

All she could see outside were trees, stretching high above them. There was a judder as the barge gently hit the side of the canal. The woman switched the engine off, rushed past her, out of the door and onto the deck, where she expertly looped the rope into a metal ring set into the wall. Cat could see that they were on the opposite side from the towpath, at a wide and lonely part of the canal.

Back in the cabin, the woman closed the door behind her, switching a small light on. She picked up Cat's phone. Her face showed nothing, though her thin hands shook a little. She was tall, slim, reedy, her legs – like a leggy spider's – folding beneath her as she sat on a chair beside the table.

"Stay where you are, where I can see you." And she did look at Cat – stared, in fact.

"What have you done to my mum?" Cat's voice

sounded loud in the small space.

"She's tied up."

Not worse then. Someone would find her. Her mum would be fine. Cat held onto that, not knowing if she could trust the woman, but needing to. So needing to.

A squashed cigarette packet lay on the table beneath the lilies. The woman threw it into a bin and took a packet out of her pocket. The knife lay beside her on the table. With the phone. Out of Cat's reach. Unless she moved very quickly. But her captor would get there first. The woman lit a cigarette and drew deeply on it.

"Do you smoke?"

"No."

"No doubt you think it's a disgusting habit."

Cat said nothing.

"Yes, well, I will smoke if I want to. This is not a public place."

Cat still said nothing. She tried to think of every story she'd ever read, every film she'd ever seen, where someone is kidnapped. Does the victim keep quiet? Or engage the captor in conversation? Should she agree with everything? Should she try to argue the woman out of whatever her plan was, or should she just go along with everything and wait for a moment to escape?

She had no idea. Her mind was frozen. She hunched her shoulders up suddenly, wrapped her arms round herself. The woman's hand jerked towards the knife. And then relaxed.

The cold was in Cat's bones. Her skin was clammy,

soaked from the rain and sweat. Icy wet denim stiffened round her thighs. Her coat had given her some protection at first but now it too felt wet. The tiniest movement made the cold feel worse as another part of her body touched sodden garments.

"Why are you doing this?"

The woman did not answer immediately. Cat looked at her face properly. The scar was worse than she'd thought when she first saw it. Small but white and raised. Dark bags dragged her eyes down. She looked … Cat wasn't sure. Scared. Sad. Fragile. And yet, she had a knife. It was impossible not to think about that knife. It was sickeningly physical.

The woman dragged deeply on her cigarette and slowly blew the smoke. Her hand was shaking more now. She reached for something on a low shelf just behind her. A packet of tablets. She pushed two out onto her hand and swallowed them without water. Pressed her fingers hard against her forehead.

And then she spoke, her voice now soft and flat, watching Cat with eyes that barely moved. "Do you have dreams?" she asked.

"I … what do you mean?"

"Dreams. Do you dream about your future?"

"I … I suppose."

"Come on! A girl like you, pretty, talented runner and swimmer − oh yes, I know all about you. I had a comfortable life too. Dreams. When I was ten, I was going to be a dancer. And then, when I was about your age, a rich lawyer. But later what I really dreamed of was…" The woman drew on her cigarette again, her eyes narrowing. "Happiness. I had this picture of myself, married, kids, house, yellow curtains. I'd make bread at a farmhouse table. I'd have lilies, big lilies, and their smell would fill the house. I saw it so clearly I could smell it. The bread and the lilies." She kneaded the fingers of her left hand together.

"Sorry, I don't…"

"Why would you? But let me tell you this: if you have dreams, prepare to lose them. Dreams are for fools."

Cat was silent, though anger was growing inside. That this woman should claim she knew her thoughts and dreams. And be so patronizing.

The woman never took her eyes off Cat. But Cat held her own eyes steady as the woman continued. "Well, I know what you dream of. You want to be an athlete, don't you? I read it. In the paper a few weeks ago. You won some competition, broke a record. And it said you were one of Scotland's great hopes. You were going to do even better than your grandfather, some Olympic medallist I've never heard of. Well, don't assume that your hopes will come true. It's easy to think that, when you're young. Then life happens." And now the woman looked away, at the floor. She twisted her cigarette end into the table.

"You don't know!" Cat blurted the words out, stung, angry. "You don't know what I want and you don't know what will happen. Just because you…" But what? She knew nothing about this woman.

"Just because I what?" The woman's voice now was sharp.

"I don't know. You haven't told me. Are you going to tell me?" She wasn't sure that she wanted to hear, but keeping the woman talking was all she could do. If she could discover what she planned, maybe she could find a way to change her mind. If her mum was here, she'd know what to say. But she wasn't here, and nor was her dad. She was on her own. Cold, and very, very frightened. The panic threatened to choke her again. She swallowed, looked at the woman, challenging her with her eyes.

The woman spoke. "She would have looked like you, I know she would. She'd have had your hair. I'd have made her be just like you, strong and everything. I'd have given her dreams too, better dreams than mine, and I'd have followed them with her."

"Who?"

After the slightest hesitation, the woman answered, "My daughter." Cat said nothing. Waited. She knew what was coming. She could see it in the woman's eyes. Something crying out. "She died."

CHAPTER 38
TRUTH

CAT barely breathed. "How old was she?"

Now the voice was muslin soft and flat. "No age at all. She never lived. Stillborn, they call it. Unborn, I'd say. I never saw her. Sometimes they let you see them. I didn't. I couldn't. But she would have been like you, I know she would. I've watched you. I know. I just know."

"But why me? There are lots of girls like me."

"But not with your father."

"What do you mean?"

"Your father and my husband – ex-husband, pardon me – were in the Gulf, the First Gulf War. My husband was destroyed by it. Our marriage was destroyed by it. Your father destroyed him. Us. Me."

"That's…" Cat wanted to say it was ridiculous.

"After my husband came back, I had to listen to his nightmares almost every night. I watched him, drunk, ranting about what he'd seen. Once he hurled a bottle of whisky against a wall when I told him to stop drinking. The glass cut my cheek and he wouldn't take me to hospital. Well, he couldn't, could he? He was drunk. But he wouldn't let me phone. I was pregnant." The woman stroked the scar on her face.

"But my father…"

"Was the man he spoke about. Over and over. Your father was the man who did not help while my husband held his dying friend's shattered head. Your father was the man my husband blamed. And then *your father* had a daughter. When I lost my baby. The day I lost my baby, *your father* was supposed to be my doctor. But it was another doctor who looked after me while the ambulance came. Because your father was at the hospital, watching *you* being born." The woman gathered herself together. She lit another cigarette.

"And I did OK, you know. I really did. Friends helped. But my marriage broke down and that was hard too. But I really did deal with it. Until this summer." She paused. "Danny was pretty upset."

Danny! What was this?

"Danny?"

"My nephew. Ex, I suppose."

And then Cat understood. This was Uncle Walter's ex-wife.

"Walter – my ex – told me that Danny was going out with the daughter of Bill McPherson. Wasn't that amazing, he said? Walter's writing his memoirs – my idea, for him to try to deal with his ghosts – and in his research he came across an article written by … guess who? Diana McPherson. Any relation, we wondered? Of course it's a relation! It's your mother. Your mother who thinks she can pontificate about Gulf War syndrome when she knows nothing. Sod bloody all. And then I saw you. I'd been watching your house. I wanted to see you, only see you, to see what you were like. And there you were. All glowing and healthy and off to some competition or something, and your parents both getting in the car with you, and all of you just looking so damned … happy."

The woman sucked on her cigarette, her hands still now, the fingers clenched.

"But how is this going to help? Kidnapping me and hurting my mum? I'm really sorry about everything that's happened to you but … I mean, what do you want? What do you want me to do? My parents will do anything. Is it money?"

The woman laughed. Pulled the cork out of a bottle of red wine and slopped a large amount into a glass. Drank from it, three large mouthfuls.

"Can I stand up?" asked Cat.

"No. Stay where you are." The viciousness had come back into her voice.

"But I've got pins and needles," lied Cat. "It's really bad. Please. I won't do anything, I promise." She lied again. She didn't know what she was going to do, but she wanted to be ready for whatever it was. Like getting into position for a race.

"You can go and lie on the bed."

Cat began to stand up, careful not to make any sudden movements. The woman stood too, watching her closely.

And then Cat's phone rang.

It sounded shockingly loud. Grabbing the knife, the woman glanced at the phone. The familiar name glowed on the screen.

"Danny!" she exclaimed, leaving the phone where it was. "Leave it!"

The woman had drunk the first glass of wine and now poured her second. She leaned on the edge of the table, still standing. Her breathing was fast and she chewed her lip whenever there was no cigarette there. Cat's eyes were stinging in the smoke. When the woman started playing with the knife, Cat had to speak, to fill the silence and try to calm the woman down. Cat was still standing too, as though about to sit on the bed. The woman seemed not to have noticed.

"What … what do you do now? To earn a living, I mean?" It was hard to keep her voice steady.

"Computers. I design websites. Computers are easy to understand. They are predictable. I could hack into any computer network you wanted me to. Got my own wireless connection." She pointed over to a corner, where Cat now saw a laptop.

"Phiz!" she exclaimed.

"Oh yes. Phiz. You shouldn't give so much of yourself away on your public space, you know. Most people use their pet's name as a password, combined with some simple system. You're no different from anyone else. Polly is your dog – it says so on Phiz – and Polly is part of every password you create. Right? I knew about your hobbies from Danny, but even if I hadn't, it's all there on the site."

Cat didn't bother to nod. It was shockingly obvious. Not David, after all. Walter had been right.

She was just about to ask something else, when the boat lurched and the wine glass slid towards her. There was the slow roar of a boat going past and then disappearing.

Cat did not plan what happened next. Survival instinct took over. She grabbed the curtain behind her and the metal pole came down. She grasped it and held it out, like a sword. It was only about fifty centimetres long and there wasn't room to move properly, but she had the advantage – the pole was longer than the knife. Not by much, but enough.

Driven by fear, she lunged at the woman, who leapt back with a furious shout. Then the woman hurled herself forward, slashing wildly with the knife. Cat forgot everything she'd been taught by Mr Boyd and let instinct take over. She parried and lunged, turning slightly all the time until her back was at the door. The woman's eyes were blurred with tears, her mouth open in desperation. Cat didn't care, couldn't care about this woman's tears.

She needed to open the door. She had no idea if it

was on a latch or if the woman had locked it. She just couldn't remember. If she pushed it and it didn't open, she was trapped. And even if it opened, the woman would come through only a second later.

For many moments, Cat delayed, parrying repeatedly, never taking her eyes from the ugly knife. And then, taking a deep breath, she lunged forward, hurling the pole like a spear at the woman, hitting her in the chest, and then darted to the door, grabbing the handle and slamming it downwards. For a moment it held, and then she was through, almost falling onto the motorbike leaning on the tiny deck. She slammed the door behind her, giving herself an extra two or three seconds.

Cat could see the far bank and the towpath some metres away. She took a deep breadth. No time to think. No choice. She jumped into the foul water.

As she jumped, a terrible cry rang out behind her. Not anger but raw desperation.

"No! Don't go! Don't go! I only wanted to…"

CHAPTER 39
RUNNING FOR LIFE

THE water was thick. And shallow. Her feet sank straight into the mud on the canal bottom, until she was up to her knees in it, unable to move forward. Her shoulders were just above the water. She needed to get her feet out of the mud and swim properly. Desperately, she ripped her coat off and left it floating behind her. Then tugged one foot out of the silt, threw herself horizontally onto the water and struggled frantically to pull the other leg out. Afraid of the foul pollution, she kept her mouth tightly closed. Each time she opened her mouth to gasp air, the brown liquid trickled inside her lips. She spat.

Only the strength in her swimmer's arms allowed her to pull her legs free. Anyone else might have wanted to keep their feet on the bottom, but she would never have been able to move. Only swimming would save her.

All too aware of the sound of the engine starting up,

the vibrating of the water, the woman shouting for her to come back, she threw every ounce of strength into fighting her way to the bank.

The woman was shouting something. But Cat could not think about that. Her own terror came first, her own need to be safe, to get home.

Her jeans were heavy and weighed her down, though she had lost her shoes in the mud. Ignoring the cold, the stink, the sounds behind her, she took a huge breath and flung her arms into a laboured crawl. She would not breathe or open her eyes – it was only about thirty metres at the most. Never had she had to work so hard to power through the water, but within less than a minute she was wading through silt and reeds, clambering up the side onto the bank. Dripping, shivering, spitting, she let out a sob as she gasped for breath. With the back of her hand she wiped the mud from her face and gagged. Gritty water caught on her teeth and she spat repeatedly until she could spit no more.

The towpath was narrow here, backed by a high wall. No escape. She looked behind her. The barge was nearly at this bank. She could just make out the figure of the woman at the helm. Hear her voice but not her words. She didn't want to hear her words.

She ran, pummelling the air, cold wind in her throat, rain running down her face, pain in her lungs. Straining to hear any sounds behind her. No sound of the boat, not any more. It must be at the bank. The woman would be leaping off. She would be only seconds behind.

Cat was fast and fit, but she was wet and horribly cold. The path was pitted and slippery with puddles of rainwater. But she ran, because it was all she could do, pounding the ground, ignoring any pain, trying to use every muscle as she'd been taught, squeezing each iota of power, arms grasping the air, head down, body forward, streamlined, forcing the ground away with each footstep.

The darkness was mustard-tinged and watery. No lights on the towpath, just straggling reflections from distant houses on the far side, their long back gardens sloping towards the canal. If anyone happened to be looking out at the right moment, they might see her running. But then what would they do? They'd think she was a jogger. Or if they were worried, she'd be gone before they could phone the police. But maybe, just maybe someone would. She should scream – but she couldn't, needed all her breath for running.

She didn't look behind her.

No one was ahead of her, no friendly late-night dog-walker – the weather was keeping everyone indoors.

And then, faintly at first, Cat heard it. She couldn't tell at first whether it came from behind her or in front. But there was no mistaking what it was.

A motorbike.

CHAPTER 40
MOTORBIKE

NOW Cat screamed as she ran. Gasping, her eyes wide, summoning every bit of strength. If she could reach the next bridge in time, she could hide. But only if she got there before the woman saw her.

She was beginning to tire. Her legs were growing heavy. It seemed like hours since she'd eaten anything. It was frightening how fast she was running out of fuel. Body diesel, as her coach called it.

The bridge was visible now. A few more seconds. The motorbike still distant enough, but definitely behind her. Approaching fast.

The noises of the city had disappeared into the sounds of the storm: the rain, the wind rattling the branches, roaring in her ears. It was impossible to imagine people sitting in front of televisions, or going about their bedtime routines, drinking hot milk, having petty arguments.

Still Cat ran, though more slowly now. She'd once

imagined she could run for ever if she wanted to. Now she knew better. Only in her dreams could she run for ever.

The bridge. She darted underneath and immediately swerved to the right, into the sheltered corner on the other side. Gasping and heaving, she squeezed herself tight against the wall. The biting wind whipped through her hair, through her thin wet jumper, through her skin.

And she waited. The motorbike was coming quickly nearer.

There was no need for her to quieten her breathing. The woman would never hear her over the sound of everything else. She would go past. Then Cat would have to run up into the open park beside the canal. Would the woman guess what had happened, when she did not quickly find Cat on the towpath? After all, the woman would know the canal better than anyone. Cat knew there'd be very little time before the woman realized what had happened and came after her.

She held her breath as the roar of the motorbike swelled. She could scream now and no one would hear at all, so loud was the noise. And then, in a black flash, it was past. Cat could make out the figure of the woman hunched over the handlebars. Her hair flew out behind her: she was wearing no helmet.

And she was gone. As Cat waited for a few more moments, anger grew in her, more than fear. "Some Olympic medallist I've never heard of," the woman had said of her grandfather. And how contemptuous she'd been of Cat's ambitions. What did she know, loser that she was, sad weirdo woman in a boat? Anger gave her strength.

A few seconds later, Cat slipped up the slope away from the canal path, her feet hurting. There was the open park, mostly playing fields, unlit, empty. And if she could cross it, she'd be at the road and could find her way home through the streets. She would be safe – or safer than by the canal.

She didn't know how long she'd have before the woman came back. But she slid into the darkness of the park, her heart thumping. The quickest way would be to go straight across the middle, but the edges looked safer.

She set off along one side, straining her ears to hear any sounds above the storm.

And now the sound of the motorbike came again in the distance.

She ran over the slippery ground. Along the edge of the trees. Gasping, breathing through rain. Fuelled by fear. Nothing mattered now. Not the cold, the rain, the pain in her feet, nothing except getting away from this maniac. She ran faster, new strength coming from somewhere.

A light swept the darkness behind her. The headlight of the motorbike. Surely someone would see now, or hear? There were buildings on the far side of the park, maybe three hundred metres away – flats where *surely* someone would be looking out. Or someone would be walking home from a takeaway or a late shift or something. Anyone.

But why *would* anyone be there, in pitch-dark, in the middle of playing fields and waste ground, on such a night? And even if someone looked, they would not see her against the trees and bushes. But the woman would see her. Because she knew what she was looking for, and had the lights of her motorbike.

The light came nearer, playing backwards and forward across the open space, searching for her.

Now the ground all around was flooded with sudden brightness as the bike came straight towards her. She had been seen. Cat stopped running, twisted round, trying to see which way the bike would hit her, which way she should jump.

The light was blinding, everywhere, enormous. She was paralysed.

With a shocking, violent roar, the bike sliced past. It went a few metres beyond her and then stopped, swung round with a spray of mud and a screech of brakes. Someone jumped from it, shouting at her through the rain and wind, words she couldn't hear over the noise of the engine, the ringing in her ears, the wind. She turned and ran. She knew she couldn't escape but all she could do was run. Sliding in the mud and the wetness, she sped away again. Running for her life.

CHAPTER 41
DAVID

"CAT! Stop!"

She stopped and turned. It was Danny, running towards her through the mud, the motorbike coming along behind him, ridden by someone who was obviously not the woman.

"Where is she?" he shouted.

"Phone for help, Danny! There's a woman chasing me on a motorbike! She…"

"I know! Your dad called the police. David and I didn't wait."

Over his shoulder, she could dimly see the figure on the motorbike, dressed in black, helmeted. David.

"Get on the bike, Cat. David will take you home. Hurry!"—

"What about you?"

The sound of another motorbike. From the canal. Cat peered through the night – there was the light far away, growing. In another distance she could hear a siren – police or ambulance, she never had learned to tell.

Danny shouted, "She's not interested in me. The police'll be here soon. Just hurry!"

But it was too late. The motorbike was roaring towards them and Cat had no time to jump onto the bike behind David.

Suddenly David shouted above the screaming of the engines, "Both of you, stand clear! Get away!" He gunned his engine into fury and the bike surged forward, back wheel spinning in the mud.

Danny grabbed Cat and pulled her into the trees.

"Is my mum OK? God, I've been so scared!" And her teeth, her whole jaw, started to shake so that she could barely speak.

"She'll be OK. She was tied up but she's fine. Shit, what's he doing?"

David was heading straight towards the other motorbike. The two lights converged, twisting this way and that like lasers as each rider tried to work out the direction of the other. One thing was clear: David was trying to drive the woman away from Danny and Cat. The two bikes came dangerously close, sliding in the mud, roaring their engines. The woman's hair was loose behind her. She looked small on the huge bike, overpowered by the black night sky.

Her bike swerved and came hurtling towards Danny and Cat. They shrank further into the trees and Cat found herself gripping Danny's arm as they tried to make themselves as small as possible behind a tree trunk.

At the last moment, just before it would have crashed into the trees, the bike curled away, and they watched the woman speed towards one of the entrances to the canal path. There she slithered to a halt. David had stopped his bike some distance away. He turned off his headlight and suddenly they couldn't see him.

The woman turned her light off.

Cat could hear her own breathing now, feel her heart racing.

The silence was short-lived. Sirens now, very close, and the park was flooded with searchlights from a police car and two – no, three – motorbikes heading towards them.

Cat felt her legs go numb and she began to fall. Danny held her upright and she quickly pulled herself together, though her feet did not seem to want to move. She must not collapse now. In the confusion of noise and lights she could not see what was happening but her brain was shutting down – she did not need to know. She was safe. She didn't *feel* safe, but she must tell herself that she was. With the danger over, she felt, if anything, more horrified. At what had so nearly happened. Still fear chilled her, still the smell of the canal choked her, still the cries of the woman as she jumped from the barge haunted her. But she must be safe now. Holding onto that thought, she fought her fear away. It was as if she was curling into herself, making a shield so that terror could not get her.

She heard someone talking to her. A policeman was there, holding out a silvery blanket. She let herself be wrapped up and led to a car that had appeared over the grass. She couldn't count the lights and people.

She was aware of David talking to a police motorcyclist, pointing. And then two motorbikes roared towards the canal. Another went in a different direction.

Cat refused to care. She refused, pushing the thoughts away, barring the doors of her mind against the cries of the woman as Cat had jumped from the boat.

Now the cold hit her, seeping into her bones. No strength was left in her. She was sitting inside the police car – how had she got there? She didn't remember sitting down.

The car pulled off and someone fastened her seat belt.

A voice was saying reassuring things. Someone was talking about how they'd seen her running, and how fast she was. No one was asking her any questions. They didn't seem to need to know anything. She didn't know anything anyway.

Someone told her she'd been very brave. How did they know? She hadn't done anything. She'd just run, and swam. And fenced! A smile twitched her lips Hysteria welled up in her and she began to laugh. If Boyd could have seen her! Or her coach!

Danny was next to her in the car. Probably thought

she was mad. Mad! He could talk! Insects, schizophrenic brother, crazy uncle...

But Danny and his schizo brother had saved her. And her hysteria shrank away into a tight dark knot of fear again.

And what if the police didn't catch the woman? What then?

CHAPTER 42
CURLING UP

THE next hour tangled in Cat's mind. Strangers in her house: police, in uniform and plain clothes, she didn't know how many. Angus's frightened face, his saxophone and music case lying on the stairs. Polly being shouted at to go to her bed. The phone ringing twice. Or more. A discussion about whether she had to go to hospital to be checked over, and her dad saying she'd be better at home.

Having to give her clothes to a policewoman, for some reason she didn't understand but which was "procedure". That must have been after her bath. Or before, she didn't know. The policewoman told her to call her Abbie, but Cat didn't call her anything. Later, her feet stinging and bleeding, before being dried and bandaged by her dad. Warm air around her and yet the bitter cold inside her, waves of shivering that overwhelmed her.

Sometimes she could not take in a full breath and she

felt she would suffocate if she did not. Every now and then her heart leapt and raced on a journey of its own, and she would gasp in sudden fear.

Metal mud taste and the smell of canal.

When she closed her eyes, she saw the woman's face, her shaking hands, tasted the cigarette smoke drifting around her. She saw tears in the woman's eyes. But had there really been tears? She didn't know for sure, only that she saw them now, in her mind where truth was blurred.

People asked her questions but, when she tried to answer, the words stuck. She didn't want to think about it. Like a cut, it needed some time to heal before it could be touched without pain.

At some point the doorbell rang and perhaps more police came and people were whispering things she had no desire to hear. The one called Abbie was talking quietly to her parents and making notes but Cat wasn't interested in trying to listen. In her mind she focused on three things only: getting warm, washing the canal filth off her, and curling up in bed with the duvet over her head.

There was the steamy warmth of the bathroom. Her own face staring like a ghost from the misted mirror. Her mum had told her to shower before she bathed, to get the worst of the dirt off, and she did. As she stood under the power jets, washing the stinking mud from her skin and hair, watching the steam curl into the air, and the brown and bloodied water swirling around her feet, she cried. At one point she almost began to sink into a crouching position in the shower, but at the last moment she caught a glimpse of herself in the shiny chrome of the shower unit, and was shocked at her own face and its look of sadness. She pulled herself together and stood up straight again, letting the hot water do its work.

Afterwards, clean at last, she climbed into the bath and let the soapy waters cocoon her. Her skin tingled painfully but bit by bit her body relaxed and drifted into warmth. The stinging on the soles of her feet softened quickly as whatever her mum had put in the water took over. Besides, it was a pain that was bearable.

The noises of the house, family and strangers, jangled outside the bathroom. In here, all was warm and misty and soft. She closed her eyes. But when she did, she saw the woman's face. Cat still did not know her name, she realized. What would happen to her? She opened her eyes.

Why should she care? But she did. A thought struggled to be voiced. In the secrecy of the bathroom, clouded, safe, selfish, honest, Cat whispered her thought aloud: "I hope she dies. Because I need to feel safe. I hope she falls off her bike into the canal and drowns."

But Cat also hated the thought of the woman dying. She remembered the sound of her cries. As if she was being deserted. The woman's dreams had ended the moment Cat jumped into the canal.

But no – her dreams had ended years ago.

At some point Cat got out of the water and wrapped herself in a towel, sitting for a few moments on the edge of the bath and watching the bubbles softly pop and fizz and burst. After a while, she left the warmth and safety of the bathroom.

Out there her mother was waiting, just sitting on the stairs. Her eyes were red, and she looked at Cat with a broken smile as she stood up.

"I've made your room warm," she said. "And you don't have to give a statement to the police till tomorrow. The nice one called Abbie will come back with detective somebody."

Cat didn't remember walking up the stairs to her room but she must have done. There was her dad, with bandages and cream to deal with her scraped feet. Her mum had brought a mug of tea for her and Cat drank its strange sweetness as she sat slumped on the bed and let herself be looked after. Soon her dad went downstairs to talk to the police some more and Cat was where she wanted to be: curled up in bed, one hot water bottle clutched between her feet and one against her stomach.

She wanted to talk to her mum, but first a doctor came and checked her over and gave her an injection for something. She didn't know if he was from the police or not, but she didn't care. He was a cold, thin man, grey-haired and greasy. She was glad when he went.

Only then could she ask what she had to ask. "Are you OK, Mum? What did she do to you?"

"Nothing. She just tied a piece of string from one finger of my bad arm to the end of the bed. That was all she needed to do. If I moved the pain was terrible.

My other hand was tied to something else. And I was gagged."

"I was so scared," whispered Cat, squeezing her eyes shut. Her mother stroked her hair.

"So was I, Catty. When I heard our door slam shut and I knew that she had got you, I … I can't tell you. I wanted to scream but I…"

Cat interrupted. "So what happened? With Danny and his brother? How come they found me?"

"Danny was brilliant. Are you back together with him, by the way?"

"No way! He's just a friend."

"Well, he's a good friend. And his brother." She hesitated.

"I know David is a patient of yours, Mum."

"Well, maybe, but you know I can't talk about that. Anyway, Danny hasn't had time to tell us everything but it's something to do with his uncle? You'd been with Danny at his uncle's or something – oh and by the way, I don't call that being "at a friend's house", which is what you'd told us… Anyway, Danny went back to get his phone, he said. Well, after that he came past here and thought it was weird that the house was all dark when he knew you were in. He rang the bell, and he tried phoning you but there was no reply. Ran back to his uncle or phoned or something and then… Anyway, you heard the rest downstairs."

"What?"

Her mum looked at her. "The police told us. You

were there. Oh, Catty, maybe you were too shocked to take it in. Well, Danny must have told the police a lot of stuff in the car, and the police also talked to his uncle. But Danny and David had gone to the canal even before the police got here. And I gather you know now – who she was? I still can't completely believe why we ended up at the centre of this, why you, but I think I'm beginning to. Bit extreme, I must say. The sort of thing you read about, something from a film. But the uncle seems decent – he's really cut up about it."

Cat's head was spinning. "You met Danny's uncle? But…"

"When David and Danny went off on the motorbike, he came round here. He was very agitated even though at that stage he didn't know everything that was happening. He'd already called the police, who were about to break in here when Dad and Angus arrived."

Cat wondered if her parents knew what Danny's uncle's opinion of them was. Did he know all along what his ex-wife was doing? She was too tired to ask about that now.

Terribly tired. Her eyes would hardly stay open. But she tried to concentrate. She'd missed something.

There was something she wasn't being told.

CHAPTER 43
SOME TRUTHS

AND then she realized. Eyes wide open now, Cat knew what she was missing, the thing she hadn't been told.

"You said 'was'."

"Sorry?" asked her mum.

"You said I knew who she *was*."

Her mother looked away. Didn't answer. Stroked Cat's head.

"She's dead, isn't she?" asked Cat.

"Yes, sweetheart. The news came while you were in the bathroom."

"How did she die?"

"It's best not to think about it."

"I need to know."

Her mother hesitated. "You know where the canal goes along the aqueduct, over the road?"

"Oh, God, she fell over the edge."

Silence.

"Did she, Mum? Did she die instantly? Please say she did."

"She did, Catty. Definitely."

Silence hung between them.

"Was it because of the police chasing her?"

"It was an accident. Apparently a man was out walking his dog in the rain and he was walking along the towpath. But you know how, at that bit, there's hardly room to pass? If the woman hadn't gone over the edge, she'd have hit the man and his dog. And that would have been her fault."

"So she did it to save him."

"She would hardly have had time to think. But if she had gone the other way she could be up for murder or manslaughter now."

"That's horrible," said Cat.

"It means we don't have to worry about her any more. I'm sorry, but I am relieved."

"I shouldn't have left her. It's my fault. If I hadn't left her, she wouldn't have…"

"No, if you hadn't left her I don't like to think what would have happened."

"She was sad though. She went on about her dreams."

"It's NOT your fault, Catty. You can't be responsible for what a fully grown adult does."

Cat shivered, pulled the duvet more tightly round her. The woman had paid a heavy price for what she'd done, and Cat could only feel horribly relieved.

Her mum continued, "Besides, she'd been spying on us. She shouldn't have done that."

"Mum?"

"Mmm?"

"I have to tell you something."

"What?"

"You know Phiz?"

There was a pause. "Yes."

"You know how she was an expert with computers?"

"No."

"Well, she was. And she did something horrible to me with Phiz."

A pause. "You aren't meant to use Phiz."

"I know. That's why I couldn't tell you before. But everyone does it."

"Oh, *everyone*?"

"Yes, actually."

"Well, it serves you right, you silly girl. What did she do?"

"She put a virus on my laptop." No need to mention the insects.

"God, Catty, have you ruined it? You idiot! They're expensive things!"

"No, Marcus and Ailsa sorted it out. It's totally fine now."

"Marcus and Ailsa … oh, for goodness' sake!"

There was a knock on the door and Angus came in. "Mum, the police are going now and they want to talk to you."

When she'd gone, and Angus too, Cat lay in her bed. Her room was filled with the smell of home. Warm, fuggy, the shutters firmly closed. Clothes had been tidied and folded neatly. Her mum always found that keeping things neat helped her feel in control. When she was stressed, she tidied. Anyway, her broken wrist had not stopped her, and now everything was very neat in her daughter's room.

Cat listened to the sounds of the house below her. The storm still blew outside, rattling the slates, whistling in the chimney.

Then, restless, she got up, her legs a little wobbly, bandaged feet sore. She hobbled over to her window, opened the shutters, and stared out.

The rain had almost stopped. The clouds were thinner, the moon shining through a gap. Between the bare branches of the trees, she could see buildings, stars, and the lights of windows.

She watched them. They were familiar. She liked them.

Cat turned round and saw her training kit, which was still waiting for tomorrow, although she knew she wouldn't need it. She crouched down and touched her running shoes, loving the soft worn leathery feel, imagining herself speeding along the track with the wind behind her. Beating everyone else. She wanted that again. Needed it. It was her. And it wasn't supposed to be easy, because then everyone would want to do it.

She would do it again. She would probably do it as

a career. Or at least go as far as she could. For as long as she wanted. It wasn't really Danny and David who'd saved her life that evening – though she would always be grateful to them. It was her running, her swimming, her strength.

There was no photo of her grandfather in her room. There should be. She wished there was. In the morning, or soon anyway, she would find out more about him. Maybe they had letters or something. Maybe he'd even kept a diary. She wanted to know about him. "Some Olympic medallist I've never heard of." Was that what she would be one day? It was a sentence that summed up the whole thing: the highs and the lows. But Olympic medallist would be worth the lows. Worth the risk. And if the point was the feeling inside her, the delicious sensation of winning, not whether some sad woman had heard of her, then that would be enough.

It was as she was about to go back to bed that she saw it – a large spider scuttling across the floor. Although at first she gasped and her hands flew to her mouth, only a second later she picked up the running shoe and hurled it at the spider.

Dead.

CHAPTER 44
MORE FLOWERS

A strange warm breeze blew as Cat walked home from the bus with Bethan, Ailsa, Josh and Marcus the following Thursday. November now, dark after school, and the weather should be cold and sharp.

It was nearly a week after she had been kidnapped and the memory was still strong. But it would fade. Her mum had told her it would shrink into something manageable. She could keep it in a part of her mind and as long as she realized that any time she wanted to talk about it, she could, that would be fine.

Still, in moments of silence or when she was alone, she found her mind taking her back to details of that night: the smell of the woman's leather jacket, the mud that clutched at her ankles when she jumped in the canal, the roar of the motorbike behind her. And the woman's desperate voice. Danny's uncle had come round, looking sad now himself. He'd talked to her parents and she didn't know what had been said, but they'd all shaken hands as he left.

At school, no one knew quite what to say. She'd been in the newspapers and people wanted more details. But there was Danny and everyone knew the woman had been his aunt. A couple of times someone had said she was a loony, and Cat had leapt to her defence, angrily. That was something they couldn't understand, why she would do that when the woman had held a knife to her. But she was just a sad woman, said Cat. A wrecked life. Doesn't mean you have to go round kidnapping people, said someone. And that was the popular view. Cat couldn't be bothered to explain. Wasn't quite sure she understood herself, but she knew what she felt.

She'd talked to her grandmother on the phone. And was going to go round soon to see letters and newspaper cuttings about her grandfather. There was a diary, her grandmother had said. "Maybe you'd like to read it? He always said if he had grandchildren they could read it. It's not a secret. I didn't know if you'd be interested. But he'd have been very proud of you, Catty."

But she didn't mind that now. It was just a phrase. And probably even true. And besides, she was proud to have a grandfather who'd done what he did. Because she knew something of what it had meant, what it had cost.

She'd given a statement to the police. It hadn't been as bad as she'd thought – they'd been very kind, a woman and a man who'd come to the house so she didn't have to go to the police station. Her parents had had to give a statement too.

On the Wednesday, they'd had fencing. Back to normal. But not completely – Mr Boyd was probably surprised to see Danny and Cat chatting as they got ready.

"How's your uncle?" Cat asked Danny. Not, frankly, that she cared too much about Danny's uncle. OK, so his wife had died, but she still found him disconcerting and slightly creepy.

"He's OK, I think. My mum's been there quite a lot. She's really sad because Sheila was her friend but at least she knows now that Uncle Walter actually did care. But she seems to have made it up with him. She told me she felt really bad not making an effort to see both sides. It's funny how it takes someone dying for adults to see sense."

Cat pulled on her glove. "Yeah, you never know – my dad and your uncle could get to discussing the war together. Two old-timers."

"I can't see them becoming best friends. Not much in common, what with my uncle's socialist principles."

"Whereas you and I have got *so* much in common!" And Cat grinned. "Insect boy!"

"On guard!" he said. They put on their masks and fought a brief but one-sided fencing bout. Danny was no match for Cat, especially when she was determined, and he knew it. As they took their masks off and saluted each other in the proper way afterwards, he smiled at her. The cute smile she'd once fallen for. It was a long time since she'd seen it.

"For a princess, you're a pretty tough fighter!"

She wouldn't have a problem with Danny again, she knew. And was relieved. They'd never be together again, not in that way – once an insect collector, always a weirdo – but he'd saved her life, or liked to think so. And she was happy to give him credit for that. As long as he didn't start getting ideas. A cute smile does not on its own make a boyfriend.

On Thursday evening, Cat arrived back home and was making a snack in the kitchen when the doorbell rang. A few moments later, her mum called her to the door. It was Danny and David. Smartly dressed from the funeral.

They'd brought flowers.

David was thin, haunted-looking and nervy, not really looking at her properly. Cat didn't mind that as the idea of him still made her uneasy, even though her mum had reassured her that he wasn't a danger.

He shook Cat's hand as he handed her the flowers, and said he was sorry. And he did smile at her, so presumably his voices had stopped telling him that she was bad.

David pointed at the flowers, shyly. "They're kind of for your mum and you," he said. "From me and Danny."

"Thanks, they're lovely," Cat said. "Any spider in them?"

"What?"

"Well, actually, Danny, I've been meaning to ask you about that. Thing is, the last time I got flowers, a massive spider fell out, and I was wondering…" She looked from one to the other.

"You thought I did it? Why would you think I'd send you flowers?"

Yes, it did seem a bit ridiculous, come to think of it.

"Forget it," said Cat.

She spent some time in the kitchen with Danny and David, talking about this and that, eating biscuits, being annoyed by Angus, who had been horribly nice to Cat ever since the drama of the previous week.

And then Danny and David left and Cat saw them to the door, watching as they disappeared. She was about to go back inside, when Polly came charging out of the house, chased by Angus.

"God, Angus!" snapped Cat, stepping backwards to avoid him.

As she did so, she knocked into a large plant pot and it fell. Leaves had collected behind.

She was just about to put the pot back in its place when she saw a dirty white card half hidden under the leaves. In an envelope. From Blooms. Angus was still running round turning Polly crazy with excitement.

She read the words aloud: "Brilliant kid! Congratulations! Mr T."

Her coach!

Cat grinned as she went indoors. She stuck the card on her noticeboard. It wouldn't be the last.

CHAPTER 45
THE WATCHER
– FINAL CHAPTER

JANUARY. The sky from his window has the quality of pearl. This early morning, each branch of the tree that taps on his window is edged with frost, like glitter on the Christmas cards that still sit on his shelves.

New Year's Day. The streets silent, sleeping, exhausted.

His book is finished. He wrote the last chapter last night, as people drank and danced the old year out, as the new one lurched its way into bleary sight. Fuelled by a special coffee – his Christmas present from Danny, as it happens – he had ground out the final words in a detached, heady haze. And then he had slept deeply.

It feels like closure. Though he will forget neither the war nor that awful, more recent night. He remembers looking out of his window that evening, after Danny had collected his phone and disappeared again. He remembers David coming home on his motorbike and then Danny rushing round once more, in a state, pressing the doorbell and shouting that something had happened. He remembers putting two and two together and, in terrible realization, making four.

Sending David off to the canal and Danny insisting on going too, rushing round to the McPherson house and calling the police when he couldn't get a reply, and then confusion, fear, sirens splitting the air, questions. And then the relief when Cat was found safe.

Followed by that shocking, spearing moment when he heard that Sheila had died. He remembers his legs almost giving way, the breath being sucked from him. And, from then on, such a cascade of mixed emotions. And unanswered questions, including the biggest: what if?

But there was no point, ever, in asking that question. Because you'd spend your life never finding the answer.

So he wouldn't. He'd written down his past and it was a real part of him. But "what if?" was not part of the past, the present or the future. It was a hopeless nothing.

And now, on New Year's morning, the start of a new future, Walter makes a small decision. He will drive out to the coast, to a beach he and Sheila used to go to. He will scatter her ashes across open water. And he will say goodbye and sorry in the only way he can, because every other way is too late and too meaningless.

As he stands up, stretching, his eye is caught by the Christmas present he had given himself.

He takes the lid off the large plastic box. Very large plastic box. There, among the moist leaves they both sit. The female is his favourite, huge, glossy black, her dozens of segments sitting perfectly, almost seeming to breathe as she moves. She uncurls herself from her coil and begins to inch towards his hand. He lets her crawl up his fingers onto his palm, and marvels at the size and weight of her. She is magnificent, enormous, an empress among her species.

Archispirostreptus gigas. The giant train millipede.

A collection of dead insects is all very well. But there is nothing better than observing the living.

EPILOGUE

SEVEN months later. A sweat-soaked summer. The air soft and yellow and humming. Cat McPherson is going for a run. Not easy in this dripping heat when part of her wants to sit in her cool kitchen and drink iced smoothies.

But she runs. Because she wants to. Because she can. Because of what it gives her. Because it is her.

Funny though – shortly after the canal incident, her parents had started to suggest she cut back on her training. They said maybe she was doing too much, that she should keep her options open, work hard at her schoolwork, treat the athletics as a hobby, not expect too much. "Happiness is the most important thing, Catty. You have to do what *you* want."

If they'd said it weeks before, she'd have jumped at the chance. But something changed the night she ran for her life. She won't forget the woman, her sadness and her lost dreams. But Cat will not let her life be damaged by that woman's shattered hopes.

She *will* have her own dreams and hold them for as long as she can. Not because she ought to but because she wants to. Not because it's right or wrong but because it just is her. Not because of her grandfather, but *with* her grandfather, because there is a bit of him in her even though most of her is herself. And although her friendships will change as she does, they will always be friendships.

She swims a bit less now but runs more, will focus on that and not the biathlon. There is more freedom in it. Not to mention the long lean muscles rather than the big shoulders that always loomed at her from the mirror.

She's read her grandfather's diary now, touched and absorbed the yellowed newspaper cuttings, seen more photos of him, talked to her grandmother. She knows more of him now, and it's interesting, fun, tugs warmly at her heart. But it doesn't matter. Because the truth is that he was an Olympic medallist and that she never knew him. And he never knew her. Maybe some of what he felt she feels too, but she will never really know that. It is comforting and human to touch the past, but it is not everything. Or enough.

She is on her own, running for herself. But more completely so.

Along the wooded path Cat runs, seeking the shade, the thick ancient branches crowding over her, protecting, a canopy of cool.

Breathing easy, strong, smooth. Floating in absolute control. Her thoughts in another space.

She comes to a fork in the path. Now she must go up the hill or down to the lake on the right. She goes to the right. When she comes to the lake, she will swing round and go up the hill from the other side. It's a longer route. She passes a family walking in the opposite direction, the two small children arguing about being carried.

Cat doesn't like small children. They irritate her. She has no patience with them. They whinge and are spoilt. They expect everything done for them. The brat has its arms outstretched to its mother, its face screwed up.

She hopes that there will be no one by the lake. She will stop to watch the swans, do a few stretches, measure her recovery time. She can hear the buzzing of flies, the hot chitter of birds.

At first, it seems as though no one is there. As she gets closer, she sees that someone is sitting on the bench, by the water. An old man, judging from his clothes. Her heart sinks. She will have to go further round, find some space. She's not going to do stretches with anyone looking.

Closer to the man now, she thinks he's asleep. His head is slumped forward. At an odd angle. His chest curled round, his shoulders sagging, his arms hanging by his sides.

She slows down. Something is not right. In her heart she knows what it is. Yet she walks towards him, pulled there, though wishing she could run away.

The man is dead. She stretches out her hand as if to touch his shoulder, but she doesn't want to. She draws her hand back towards herself.

And then a smell. A memory. The smell of him. She knows his smell. And with that memory comes guilt and horror, all in one moment. He is the man who brought hissing cockroaches into their classroom. There is his jacket pocket, his musty smell, his tweed, his patches, his wispy hair. She will not look at his eyes, but they will be his eyes – she does not need to look.

Words rise in her throat. She turns, screams, sees a man and woman in the distance, waves, screams again. "Help! Please! This way!"

And as they hurry towards her she sees something remarkable. A thin blue insect floats through the air and hovers in front of her face. It is a dragonfly, she thinks, though of course she does not know what sort it is. Danny would know. The blue is artificial in its powdery blueness. It floats there, its buzzing almost silent. Then it settles on the man's shoulder, its wings shivering. Two pairs of wings it has, iridescent, veins of amazing thinness. It is beautiful. The most beautiful thing she has ever seen.

Cat holds out her hand towards it, her palm upwards. And the blue dragonfly lifts into the air and comes to settle on her skin.

She barely breathes. Suddenly nothing is as important as that tiny thing of beauty.

The man and woman have arrived now and they have discovered what Cat knows, that here is a dead person. The man is making an urgent call on his mobile phone: police, ambulance, hurry. The woman is looking at her strangely.

"Are you all right?"

Cat looks at her and smiles through watery eyes. Words don't come, at first. She looks at the dead man's face and she thinks how peaceful he looks now, just as though he were asleep. His mouth is set in the slightest, softest smile. Cat gently blows the dragonfly from her hand and towards the lake, where it lands on the water a little way away.

"He wouldn't have wanted it to be hurt," she says. The woman doesn't look reassured. "He liked insects," Cat continues. "He came to our school once."

"I think you should sit down," says the woman. "You don't look very well. You've had a shock."

Later that evening, when the police have taken a statement – she's good at those now – and her parents have worried about her unnecessarily, Cat goes round to Danny's house. There is something she wants to know. She describes the insect and he finds pictures in his books.

"Two pairs of wings or one? Horizontal or vertical?"

"Two. Um, horizontal, like a tiny plane."

"Sounds like proper dragonfly then, not a damselfly. Like this?"

"A bit like that but more like this one."

"What about this one?"

"Wrong colour. Mine was more sort of a pale powdery blue. And no black bit on the tail."

And then she sees it. Points to it. "That's it! I know it is!"

Danny reads out the name. "Odonata Anisoptera *Orthetrum coerulescens*."

"Odonata Anisoptera *Orthetrum coerulescens*," she repeats slowly, for the words are soothing, secret, ancient. Strong.

"Beautiful, isn't it?" he says, though it is not a question but a statement.

She touches the picture, softly, as though stroking it.

It is beautiful. She nods. No longer does she hate or fear these small things. She does not wish to spend her life with them, but she can understand a little of why someone would. Dreams, desires and obsessions come from within and are like gifts, uninvited. But she has different gifts. And different dreams.

When high-born William de Lacey saves a highwayman's life, he cannot guess how his own life will change. He may have escaped his father's sneering contempt, but has his easy childhood prepared him for the terrifying dangers that he must face now? The stark, ghostly moors are as hostile as the pursuing redcoats, and Will must make some difficult decisions if he is to escape with his life.

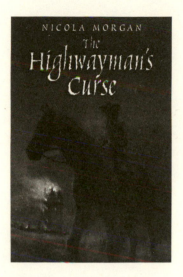

On the run from the redcoats, the two young highway robbers, Will and Bess, find themselves in Galloway, Scotland, blamed for a murder they did not commit. Captured by smugglers, they become embroiled in a story of hatred and revenge that goes back for generations, to the days of the Killing Times. As Will and Bess become entangled in the dangerous lives of this embittered family, both have choices to make which will test to the limit their courage and resolve. They may try to break the cycle of religious hatred that curses the land, but will their friendship survive?